Rowan and the Wolf

(Very, very loosely based on Little Red Riding Hood)

A standalone story by

Lisa Oliver

Table of Contents

Chapter One 7

Chapter Two 17

Chapter Three 29

Chapter Four 41

Chapter Five 55

Chapter Six 67

Chapter Seven 83

Chapter Eight...95

Chapter Nine 113

Chapter Ten...127

Chapter Eleven 147

Chapter Twelve 159

Chapter Thirteen 177

Chapter Fourteen 185

Chapter Fifteen 197

Chapter Sixteen 209

Chapter Seventeen..223

Chapter Eighteen..233

Chapter Nineteen..243

Chapter Twenty...261

Chapter Twenty-One 277

Epilogue...289

About the Author 303

Other Books By Lisa/Lee Oliver 305

Dedication

For everyone who believes in fairy tales and who, like me, hopes to find their own Happily Ever After one day.

A huge shout out and thank you hugs to Carla and Amanda for their wonderful "polishing" work. You guys are amazing.

And to my lovely readers, if this book makes you smile then my work is done – remember love beats hate every single time.

Spread the love.

Author's Note

My regular readers will recognize the first part of this story, as it was published for free through Stormy Glenn's Manlove Fantasies blog, last year I think it was. The prompt at the time was to adapt a fairy tale for MM readers and while I think the only relation to Little Red Riding Hood is Rowan's curls, and the fact there are wolves in this story, that is where the association ends. I do hope you enjoy it anyway.

Hug the one you love,

Lisa.

Chapter One

Clutching the parcel tighter under his arm, Rowan slipped through the deep shadows cast by the old buildings in the run-down neighborhood. His grandmother used to tell him stories of how safe and family-friendly the place used to be, years before when she and his grandfather first married. Now, it was a den of thieves and drug addicts all looking for their next opportunity.

There was a cackling laugh off to his right and Rowan peered over his shoulder even as he kept moving forward. His grandmother's house was just two blocks further. *I've got to get there. I won't leave her without food.* Back when Rowan's parents were killed by rogue wolves, his grandmother was the only one prepared to offer him a home. The alpha at the time had dismissed him as being too small and not worth the resources, but Rowan's grandmother had never made him feel anything but special. Even though Rowan had since gotten his degree in computer science and graphics, and moved out, he still visited every week without fail, bringing her all the food he could carry. It was the least he could do for the woman who saved him.

Just one more block to go. Rowan could almost smell the hint of his grandmother's baking in the still night air. Even though she subsisted on a meager pension the pack alpha was forced to pay on the death of her mate, Rowan's grandmother spent her days baking for the neighborhood kids who roamed the streets while their parents were sleeping off the night before. She never forced her good nature on anyone; baking huge trays of scones, nourishing muffins, and batches of cupcakes, she'd leave the trays on her stoop. Rowan had watched the kids slink like alley cats, grabbing what they could reach, but then they'd just as quickly disappear. Rogue Alley was not the place to be caught loitering even during the day.

It was all the fault of the reigning alpha who didn't give a damn about his people or how they survived.

Although gossip on the streets said the alpha's health was failing and while in normal circumstances that would be good news for the likes of Rowan and his grandmother, the alpha's son, Percy was even worse. Legends of his cruelty and sadism weren't exaggerated. Rowan still had a scar on his back from their last run in and he'd never walk without a limp again. After that incident, his grandmother begged him to stop coming. He, in turn begged her to move in with him. It wasn't as though his apartment wasn't big enough. But she stubbornly wanted to spend her last days in the house that had so many positive memories for her. He, just as stubbornly, wasn't going to leave her to fend for herself.

Which was why he only crossed town when the night was dark, leaving his car where there were still working streetlights. The bulb above his head now had been smashed out long ago, the new inhabitants of the area preferring the cover of darkness for their nefarious activities.

The sound of a rock kicked across the cracked pavement made Rowan's heart stutter and he listened intently to his surroundings. There wasn't a sound and that was never a good thing. Even on the darkest night, it was possible to hear the sounds of a child crying or the raucous drunks at one of the open house parties. But tonight, the neighborhood was silent, watchful, as though everyone knew danger lurked.

Rowan's heart beat faster. He was so close, but even as he tried to relax his breathing, a voice in the darkness made his hackles rise.

"Little wolf, little wolf, what are you doing roaming around our territory at night; all alone, in the dark, with no one to save you."

Rowan cringed. Percy's voice was the stuff of nightmares. Although the alpha's son, Percy would never be more than a beta with attitude above his station, but no one Rowan knew would ever dare say so to his face. To compensate for his lack of alpha status, Percy made sure he was the loudest and the meanest SOB in the pack.

"I'm just taking some provisions to my grandmother," Rowan turned, keeping his back to the wall. He knew there was no point in running. Percy had ensured he'd never do that successfully again. "She gives so much to the children of the pack. I just wanted to ensure she has what she needs." He clutched the parcel to his chest.

"She's not your responsibility, is she?" Percy stepped out of the shadows. The leather jacket, complete with chains and ripped jeans made the man look like a reject from a punk concert; the four goons with him adding to the scene. Rowan recognized all of them from when he was growing up. The likes of Saul and Beau were friends with him at one stage when they shared a mutual love of computer games and coding. That had been before he'd shifted. Now they were clones of the alpha's son, complete with sneers. "Looking after pack members is the alpha's responsibility. Are you aiming to challenge my father for his position, boy?"

Rowan gulped. "These are just a few special treats my grandmother had a fancy for. She'd never dream of asking the alpha for items so trivial."

"Treats?" Percy's malicious eyes gleamed as he looked at his friends. "We could certainly do with some treats, couldn't we boys? Hand them over."

Rowan squirmed but the hold on his parcel tightened. "I promised these to my grandmother. You wouldn't want me to break my promise to a sweet old lady, would you?"

"How do I know you've got treats?" Percy's bottom lip pushed out in a pout. "You could be smuggling contraband. Drugs. Booze. Blights on our territory. Hand the parcel over."

"It's nothing like that." Percy was the biggest drug supplier in the area. Police had been trying to catch him for years, but every time Percy was caught, his father made the issue go away. When Percy learned the local precinct had a revolving door for people with his last name, his behavior got worse. "You could scent it, if I was carrying drugs. Honest. I've got nothing but flour, a few eggs, and some butter."

"That's not treats," Percy scoffed. "You said treats."

"It's what my grandmother wanted. These are her ingredients so she can make treats for the kiddies. Please, she's waiting for me. I've got to go."

"I think he's lying," Percy looked across at Saul. "What do you think?"

Please, please, please, please. Doesn't our past friendship mean anything? But Saul curled his lip. "I think we should just take it from him and if he's lying, he can pay the consequences."

"I'm not lying," Rowan cried. His heart was beating so fast it felt as if it was coming out of his chest. He was struggling to breathe and the ache in his knee was a keen reminder of the last time he 'paid the consequences.'

He hadn't done anything wrong that time either, but for some reason Percy hated the fact he existed. Ripping open his package, he grabbed the bag of flour he'd bought just a few hours earlier. "See," he said, holding it up. "Baking flour." Taking a chance, he threw the bag at Percy, but Percy wasn't quick enough to catch it. Rowan could only stare in horror as the bag split open and smashed all over Percy's dark clothing.

Shit. Oh, well in for a penny, in for a pound. "Do you want the butter too? Oh, look, here's the eggs." His entire body was shaking by this time. Throwing them as hard as he could, Rowan scored a perfect hit with all six eggs. Saul growled as he wiped the dripping remains of food off the side of his face.

"You asshole," Percy screeched, looking down at his outfit. "This jacket cost me four hundred dollars."

You got ripped off. Rowan didn't voice his thoughts; he'd exhausted the last of his bravado. As Percy and the others advanced on him, he cowered against the wall, no match for wolves so much larger than he'd ever be. Closing his eyes, Rowan sent out a fervent prayer that his grandmother wouldn't come looking for him, at least until they were done. Rowan could see the rage in Percy's eyes and knew he'd gone too far. Covered in flour and dripping egg white, the situation would've been funny if he wasn't about to be killed. Closing his eyes, Rowan clamped his lips shut as he waited for the first punch.

"Percy, get away from that boy before I rip your arm from its socket."

That wasn't his grandmother's voice. Rowan's ears pricked up. No, the speaker had a voice like dark chocolate with a spicy edge. Despite the harsh tones, Rowan felt a blanket of calm move down his back and his wolf sat up and whimpered. *What the hell? That's never happened before.*

"This has got nothing to do with you, Shadow. This is a pack matter."

Percy's voice sounded shaky. Rowan risked peeking through his hands.

The stranger was h-u-g-e HUGE. Percy was blocking Rowan's view, but Rowan got the impression of tree-trunk legs and shoulders far wider than anyone he'd seen before.

"Didn't dad give you the memo, Percy?" Shadow chuckled. "He stepped down this morning and gave me the pack. You know, seeing as I'm the oldest son and the only other alpha in this family. Now, get away from my mate."

Rowan whimpered; he couldn't help it. But he didn't know what was bothering him more; the fact that Percy's face was whiter than the flour splattered on him, that the man who was now alpha of the pack was bigger than the current alpha would ever be, or...or... that no wolf ever called someone their mate unless they meant it. Peering around Percy and the others' legs, Rowan could see his escape. His grandmother's house was just down the road, her solitary porch light shining like a beacon. Ignoring the tension swirling around, he crept as quietly as he could past the legs and down the road. He needed to speak to his grandmother.

Chapter Two

Shadow could see Rowan sneaking away and smiled. His mate had survival instincts and he'd need them in the coming weeks. Besides, with Rowan out of the way for a minute, Shadow could concentrate on his scrawny brother and his cronies. When Shadow arrived, at Rowan's grandmother's insistence, he'd been horrified at what had happened to his old stomping grounds. Poverty and fear lurked on every corner - the houses all fallen into disrepair. It was as if the entire pack had lost hope.

And the reason for that was standing in front of him.

Shadow and Percy's father had lost hold of his marbles a long time ago and that was obvious from the moment Shadow stepped into the mansion he'd lived in as a child. His father hadn't showered in days, drool falling from his chin onto clothes that wouldn't be accepted at a charity shop for rags. The situation didn't take long to work out – Shadow's father was alpha in name only; it was

Percy who was running the show. Shadow could only imagine that if Percy had been born an alpha, their father would have been dead long before. But Percy needed the old man alive to keep his position.

"I don't know what you're talking about, Shadow." Percy appeared cockier than he had a right to be, but then he probably thought he was safe with his friends. "Everyone knows dad runs this pack with an iron fist. I just carry out his orders."

"Did you miss the part where I said I'd seen dad already and he stepped down as alpha?" Shadow rolled his shoulders and clicked his neck first one side and then the other. "You might have left him a dribbling mess, but he had enough sense to submit the moment he saw me."

"Bullshit." Percy stuck out his chin. "The whole pack knows I'm next in line to be alpha. They won't follow you."

"Then they can leave the territory. I don't give a shit." Shadow cracked his knuckles for emphasis. "You knew I was coming back. All of you." Staring at each wolf in turn, Shadow was disgusted none of them would meet his eyes. "Saul, Beau, I gave you a job before I left. Did you forget what I charged you to do – that you gave me your solemn promise you would do for me?"

"They follow my orders, not yours," Percy interrupted quickly.

"Hey, it's not our fault Rowan was hurt," Beau yelled. "Percy ordered the hit on him. We were just following orders."

"Hurt?" Shadow ran the sight of Rowan moving away through his mind, the boy's grandmother's warnings and urgency that he come home making more sense now. His wolf appeared in his eyes as he realized what was wrong with the picture. "He limps. Rowan wasn't limping when I left. A wolf shifter doesn't ever sustain permanent injury. They just shift and heal."

"They have to shift before the bone sets the wrong way," Saul mumbled.

"Percy held him in silver cuffs for a week after the last beating."

"Shut the fuck up," Percy shouted, slapping Saul on the shoulder. "What does it matter to you anyway? You left. Rowan is nothing but a drain on resources. He doesn't matter. He's never mattered."

Ignoring Percy, Shadow focused on Beau and Saul. "You guys were Rowan's best friends. Why didn't you tell my brother that Rowan was my omega mate and I'd left orders for him to be protected with your lives?" Shadow's claws flexed from his fingers and his fangs dropped.

"You've been gone ten years," Saul said bitterly. "Things change. Of course, we told Percy about it when the alpha got sick and he started running things, but it was clear you weren't coming back. You're lucky Rowan's still alive. If I had my way, he'd be dead. Guy always thought he was too good for the likes of us when he got his degree and created his first computer game."

"Rowan didn't want you to fuck him," Percy cackled. "You looked like such a wuss, panting after him as though he was in heat. Fucking hilarious."

Shadow slapped his fist into his open palm, silencing Saul's growl. "Enough. You've all failed. Percy, you were never going to be alpha. No beta can take over a pack. As for you, Saul and Beau. I fucking trusted you. Now my Rowan is hurt and it's all your fault."

"Rowan doesn't know he's your mate, though, does he?" Percy's laugh held a shred of hysteria. "He's run from you. Big bad alpha can't even keep his omega in line."

"I know where Rowan is," Shadow's eyes turned feral. "I wouldn't have wanted him to see this anyway. Who's first?"

Snapping out his fist, Percy's shriek pierced the air. In the carnage that followed, no one so much as stuck their nose out of their doors but the air of tension that hovered over the pack eased. By the time the last shriek gurgled away to nothing, everyone knew there was a new alpha in town. What that meant for the pack was anyone's guess, but it couldn't be as bad as it was before.

/~/~/~/~/

"Gran. Gran." Rowan stumbled through his grandmother's door.

"Oh, my stars, boy, are you all right?" Gran got up from her rocking chair, pulling her shawl around her. "Where's Shadow," she asked, peering around him. "I felt for sure he'd be with you. In fact, I didn't expect to see you at all tonight. But seeing as you're here, I'll make some tea."

She shuffled towards the kitchen and Rowan followed her. "You sent that big guy after me? Why?"

"Shadow? Of course, I sent him to look for you." Gran filled the kettle and set it on the stove. "You were late, and you know how I hate you walking around here at night." She reached up into the cupboard and pulled down one of her baking tins, setting it on the table.

Flopping into the nearest chair, Rowan stared at his gran, still trying to make sense of all that'd happened. "Who is that guy? I've never met him before."

"Of course, you have," Gran set his cup on the table and then moved over to the stove, filling her ancient teapot with the boiling water. Covering the teapot with a tea towel, she carried it over to the table. "That's Shadow, the alpha's oldest son. When you were a wee tot, you used to follow him around all over the place."

"I'm sure I'd remember someone like that," Rowan said, feeling his cheeks flush. "He's built like a giant tree."

"I have to admit that boy has grown," Gran slowly lowered herself into the chair opposite him and pushed the baking tin towards him. "Of course, he wasn't known as Shadow back then either. You'd remember him as Gray."

"Gray?" Rowan was caught between opening the tin and watching his Gran. "There's no way that mountain

I saw was Gray." Pulling open the tin, he saw butterscotch muffins, his favorite. "I mean, Gray was tall, yeah, and of course I noticed him. He was the alpha's son. But there's no way the guy I saw tonight was him, he had to be three times Gray's size. Besides everyone said when Gray left there was no way he was coming back."

Rowan didn't mention that Gray's departure had broken his heart. He'd been fourteen at the time, on the verge of his first shift. That was back in the day when he, Saul, and Beau were inseparable. Gray was the elusive, sexy adult that starred in all of Rowan's sex dreams, and in hindsight Rowan recognized he had a king-sized crush on the man. He used to spend hours practicing what he'd say to the man if he ever got the gumption to talk to him. He wrote letters he just as swiftly deleted from his computer and couldn't take his eyes off the man every time he saw him.

He remembered Gray leaving like it was yesterday. His crush had a bag slung over his shoulder, and he was already looking towards the bus. "Stay strong, kid," he'd said. Rowan still remembered the tingling sensations he'd gotten from Gray's fingers carded through his hair, how every cell in his body yearned to follow the man no matter where he went. Rowan spent six months fantasizing about Gray coming back, sweeping him off his feet and declaring his love for him in front of the pack. But then he shifted for the first time, his parents were killed, and his life officially got flushed down the toilet.

"Shadow is Gray or was Gray. I think he picked up his new name in the army," Gran said happily, pouring the tea, "and there was never any question of whether he'd come back or not. He did his time in the army, while he was waiting for you to grow up. And now he's back. Things are going to change around here and it's about time."

Rowan was just about to ask what the heck his Gran meant by her cryptic comments, when an unearthly shriek rang through the air sending shivers down Rowan's spine. "What the hell was that?" Even in the rough neighborhood, screams like that didn't happen unless someone was losing his balls to a claw.

"Language, boy," Gran reproved as she stirred sugar into her tea. "I imagine Shadow's found out just how badly Percy and his cronies hurt you and is dispensing some old-fashioned wolf justice. It's about time they got their comeuppance."

"How can you be so calm about this?" Rowan wasn't capable of hating anyone. It went against his nature as an omega and while Percy and the others had made his life hell, he accepted it as his lot in life.

Gran sighed. "There's some things I should've told you long before this, but with Percy in charge, I didn't want you to be more of a target. The fact of the matter is, Gray, or Shadow as he's known now, knew you two were mates before he left. Fated mates. You were ready for your first shift, and his older wolf could scent who you were to him. That's why he left, because you were too young to claim, and he wasn't sure he could control his urges. He told me and your parents. He even asked permission from your father to claim you when you were ready, which your dear father was happy to give. But Gray knew teenage years were hard enough for a wolf as it is, and if you'd scented him after you'd shifted, then it would've been impossible for you two to stay away from each other."

"But...but... after he left, that's when everything went to crap for me and the pack." Rowan was horrified. Before Gray left, life at the pack was relatively calm and while the alpha could be harsh, things were a lot better. Rowan didn't notice how badly things in the pack deteriorated at the time. First, he was moping over Gray leaving and then his parents died...and yeah, by the time he finally shook free his fog of grief the pack was under Percy's rule and life went downhill from there. "If Gray had stayed..."

"The alpha would've still gotten sick and Percy would've still been an ass. What happened to the pack in the last ten years isn't Gray's fault or yours. He did the right thing. Now, eat your muffin."

When his Gran put her foot down, Rowan knew better than to argue. Another shriek tore through the air and Rowan quickly stuffed his muffin in his mouth. He only hoped that the ten years Shadow spent in the army meant he knew how to incapacitate a man quickly. He wasn't going to shed a tear for Percy and his friends if they were dead, but he didn't want them to suffer.

Chapter Three

Peering through Gran's kitchen window on the side of the house, Shadow smiled at the homely scene. Gran was just as he remembered; a little older, her shoulders stooped under her shawl and the spark slightly dimmer in her eyes but the love for her grandson showed in every wrinkle and smile line. She was never a big woman and now it seemed she and Rowan were similar in height and build. Rowan, his little-red, lived up to his name. His bright red curls hung around his face like he'd never heard of haircuts. He was currently stuffing a muffin between his bright red lips. Shadow was sure Rowan was a true redhead and he was keen to find out. But even if he wasn't, that milky white skin, bright green eyes and sensuous full lips had fueled Shadow's fantasies for ten long years.

And this is it. The moment I've waited for every minute for the longest ten years in history. The bad guys were dead – at least the worst of them.

Shadow was under no illusions more would crawl out of the woodwork before long, but they'd go the same way as Percy and his cronies. His father was installed in a shifter hospital. Unfortunately, canine dementia was a thing and while he'd never heal, Shadow could relax knowing his father's last days would be comfortable. Three of his good friends, who'd all left the army the same time he did, were currently setting up the pack house for his new mate.

Shadow inhaled slowly and then quickly checked his shirt for blood splatter. He didn't want to make a bad first impression, or second, but whatever. This was it. The moment he walked through Gran's door his life would change forever. Slipping around to the back of the house, Shadow strode up the tiny back porch and knocked loudly on the door.

/~/~/~/~/

"That'll be the new alpha calling for you," Gran smiled as she stood up, clutching her shawl around her.

"Me," Rowan's voice squeaked. "Where are you going? Don't you want to talk to him?" Gran was heading down the hallway.

"I'm going to bed," Gran called out. "Don't worry about the dishes. Lock the door when you leave."

Leave. That sounded like a great idea. Rowan peered through the house to the front door. He even took a step towards it. But then a second knock sounded behind him and he knew he couldn't do it. For one thing, he'd never be fast enough to get away from the huge alpha and for another...Rowan was really keen to see if this Shadow person was Gray, just like his gran said he was.

Making his way to the back door, Rowan opened it cautiously, leaving the chain on. In this neighborhood you could never be too careful. "Hello," he said, peering around the door. He'd recognize those piercing blue eyes anywhere, although the heat in them was something new.

"Are you going to let me in, little-red?"

Rowan gulped. "The name is Rowan not that I expect you to remember," he said, closing the door enough to slip the chain off and then opening it wider.

"I've never forgotten you."

Rowan's whole body tingled under the caress in that voice, from the tips of his toes, to the ends of his curly hair, it wrapped around him like a hug. But he wasn't about to forget his place. "Please, come in, Alpha. Welcome to my grandmother's home."

"I was hoping you'd come to the pack house with me," Shadow smiled as he stayed on the back porch. "There's so much we need to catch up on."

Biting the corner of his lip, Rowan looked down at his leg. Covered with his pants, he looked like anyone else, but the moment he went to move, the alpha was going to know something was wrong with him. "Alpha, Gray, or Shadow, or whatever you prefer. I heard what you said back in the alley. You believe I'm your mate."

"I know you're my mate. I've known about it for ten long years."

"Yes, well." Shit. Rowan didn't know what to say. Mates were like the holy grail and he should be happy dancing his mate was so capable, hunky and damn, he had a lovely voice. But the reminder of why he couldn't happy dance tugged at him. He knew he had to do the right thing. "I got hurt a little while ago and now I'm permanently defective. Being with me will weaken your position. I release you from any claim you thought you might have to go through with." The words came out in a rush, but Rowan knew the alpha got the gist because he scowled and pushed through the door.

"Show me."

"Alpha?" Rowan felt like he was going to swoon. Not that he'd ever swooned before, but damn. His wolf was all excited someone so big and strong was paying attention to him and he felt his knees go weak.

"I saw you had a limp. I want to see how bad it is." Shadow made his request sound as though it was the most common thing in the world. But Rowan wasn't the type to drop his pants for anyone. Even if his wolf thought it was a good idea.

"Can't you just take my word for it?" The only reason Rowan was a twenty-four-year-old virgin was because he couldn't bear the pity or disgust from people seeing his leg. "It's not pretty."

"Do I look like someone who has a lot to do with pretty? I've seen stuff that will make your hair curl." Shadow ran his fingers through Rowan's curls eliciting the same tingling sensations as the last time the man touched him. "Although you've already got them, and they're real pretty. Please, little-red. If you are so damn sure the damage to your leg is going to turn me away, then show me. You're not giving me a chance to prove you wrong."

Rowan was sure his face was as red as his hair, but he rested his fingers on the waistband of his pants. He was torn and a huge part of him wanted to admit it. He had the man of his dreams standing in front of him – bigger, stronger and better able to protect him than anyone ever could before. And that same part of him wanted to hang onto that just a little bit longer.

But the other part – the one forged after he'd been hurt - was determined to go his own way and never be a burden on anyone. He knew he had to face his responsibilities. Shadow spent ten years believing they were mates, but that stemmed from seeing him slim and whole. Rowan wasn't that person anymore and if Shadow needed visual proof of that, then so be it.

Closing his eyes, Rowan quickly undid the button on his pants and pushed them down his legs.

/~/~/~/~/

Such a brave boy, Shadow thought as he dropped to his knees, gently tugging Rowan's pants lower. Oh, he couldn't help but notice the sweet bulge now sitting at eye level, but he needed to put Rowan's fears to rest before they went any further.

Swallowing hard, Shadow ran his hand down Rowan's right leg. His mate was lean and strong, just as Shadow envisaged. The left leg? Shadow closed his eyes for a moment as the scarring appeared and then he forced himself to open them. If Rowan thought for a second he wasn't respected, or cherished, despite his wounds, then Shadow would never get his dream claiming.

"Hmm," he said, his finger tracing over the worst of it. "Beau mentioned Percy held you for a week in silver cuffs to stop you from shifting, is that right?"

"Yes. By the time Gran got me to the pack doctor, he said there was nothing he could do. The bones had already set wrong. It was broken in three places. As you can see, one of the breaks came through the skin which is why that lump is there. He offered to amputate from the knee down, but I said no. I was walking by that stage. I've learned to live with it."

"That is amazing," Shadow stroked over the mutilated skin. It felt different, but it wasn't any worse than some of the other things he'd seen. Ten years in the army made him immune to most of life's horrors. Although, if he could resurrect Percy he would, just so he could break every bone in his brother's body and leave him to suffer, just as Rowan clearly had.

"There's nothing amazing about being hurt in a shifter world," Rowan said angrily, trying to pull away, but Shadow didn't let go. "It's a sign of weakness. People assume there's something wrong with your wolf when there isn't. But then they always thought the worst of me anyway and having a permanent limp didn't help matters."

"Does all the pack treat you as badly as Percy?" Shadow wondered if he might have to rethink his decision about taking over. He'd leave and take Rowan with him if he had to.

Rowan was giving it some thought, which was good. His omega didn't know it yet, but his answer would reflect on the future of the entire pack. "No," Rowan said at last, his voice strong despite standing in his grandmother's house with his pants around his ankles. "They weren't so bad. They just knew better than to interfere. Most of the pack are decent hard-working people who just want to live their lives in peace. Percy and his cronies didn't make that easy. But none of them were cruel unless they were pushed into it."

Relieved, Shadow allowed himself another caress as he gently pulled Rowan's pants up. Rowan bit his lip, so Shadow stroked that too. "I still want you as my true mate," he said quietly, leaning into the scent he'd dreamed of for so long. "I still plan on claiming you, the way I dreamed of doing all those lonely nights we spent apart."

"I never knew about what we could be together and even then, I used to dream about you, long after you left me that day." Rowan's hand on his face was hesitant, but Shadow's wolf howled in victory. "Did anyone tell you what amazingly big eyes you have?"

Shadow grinned. "Are you making a little red riding hood reference, little red? Because I have to tell you, you have the most beautiful curls I've ever seen and if you're looking for a big wolf to bite you, then you've come to the right place."

"Well, you have got big teeth, and I imagine your ears are impressive when you're in your shifted form." Rowan chuckled. "But I'm not wearing a red cape for anyone. It'll clash with my hair."

Levering himself to his feet, Shadow held out his hand. "Are you ready to come to the pack house with me? I promise to eat you all up and tomorrow I'll do exactly the same thing all over again."

"Just let me lock the door." Rowan led them outside and made sure the lock was down and his Gran's door was secured. "My car's over on West and Durham. You fancy a ride?"

"With you? Anytime."

/~/~/~/~/

Gran could practically hear the neighborhood sigh in relief as the two men made their way to Rowan's car. And in the house she'd shared with her loving husband for more than fifty years, Gran smiled at the picture of her long dead mate. "He finally came home," she said, as she rolled over and closed her eyes.

Chapter Four

Rowan had never been to the alpha's house, although like all pack members he knew where it was. As he stared up at the white columns fronting what could only be described as a mansion, he thought of the poverty most of the pack lived with and felt guilty for even considering going inside.

"Do you mind if I ask what happened to the old alpha?" He asked as he pulled up outside the impressive façade. "The pack were simply told he was sick, but no one had any details."

"He has canine dementia," Shadow said quietly. "Far too advanced to do anything about it now, I'm afraid. A friend of mine knew of a shifter hospital where he'll get round the clock care. He only knew me, or should I say was aware of me for a few minutes, but it was enough for him to relinquish the pack to me in front of witnesses which made things easier. I realize he was a harsh alpha, but no one should've been left in that condition for so long."

"He started leaving things to Percy about a year after you left." Rowan looked out the car window, unable to meet the intensity of Shadow's eyes. "The doctor did try and see him many times, but Percy kept accusing the doctor of trying to challenge a sick man and wouldn't let him in the house. Once Percy started dealing drugs, his group of bullying friends grew and most of the pack learned to keep their heads down and their mouths shut."

"Yes, well, Percy and his four friends I met tonight, won't cause any harm anymore."

Rowan sighed. "So much violence in this pack," he whispered, thinking of all the beatings he'd heard about and witnessed the aftermath of. "This pack never needed anyone to lord over them and force them to pull their weight. I told you, most of them work really hard just to survive. The alpha," Rowan looked down at his hands. "Sorry, Percy forced everyone to give so much to him and his friends they could barely put food on their own tables. I swear the scones and muffins my grandmother makes are sometimes the only food some of those children in Rogue Alley see in a day."

"You are a good kind-hearted omega," Shadow's hand landed like a branding weight on Rowan's shoulder. "I promise you things will get better for everyone who embraces a positive change. I can't promise that you won't see violence anymore. If people resist or want to continue trading drugs and sex in my territory, I will stop them by any means possible. But those who want a chance, will have one."

Looking up, Rowan could see the sincerity in Shadow's eyes and taking a chance, he reached up and rested his hand on top of the bigger one on his shoulder. "The people here deserve something positive for a change, but for some, old habits die hard."

"Which is why I've brought friends with me." Shadow nodded through the windscreen and Rowan noticed three burly men standing on the porch watching them. "When your grandmother sent word of how bad things had become, I offered the men I served with a chance to form my inner circle. There are two more coming in the next week. I wasn't sure there was anyone here I could trust anymore."

"You did the right thing. Most of the bigger wolves in the pack were either conscripted by Percy or driven out." Rowan worried his bottom lip with his teeth. "Do they know about me?"

"Oh yeah," Shadow laughed. "Be prepared for a bit of teasing about that. They'll try and tell you I've done nothing but talk about you for ten years."

"And did you?" Rowan turned back to the man who claimed to be his mate. "Talk about me, I mean?"

"Once or twice." Shadow showed his teeth. "Come on. Let's go inside. I'll introduce you to the guys and then we can have some privacy to get to know each other. What do you say?"

"Are you sure?" Rowan tugged at the jeans covering his bad leg. "I'm not the perfect little omega anymore. I don't want to disappoint your friends."

"You are perfect in my eyes," Shadow said with a confidence only an alpha could muster. "That's all that's important."

Oh boy, have you got a lot to learn about the changes in this pack, Rowan thought as he squeezed Shadow's hand and stepped out of the car.

/~/~/~/~/

Shadow took Rowan's keys and made sure the vehicle was locked before grabbing his hand and leading him up to the porch. He kept his pace slow, unsure how well Rowan could keep up with his usual stride. Even so, he could tell when his friends noticed Rowan's limp. The anger in the air was palpable and Rowan shivered.

"Rowan, my mate, these are three of the men I served with. On the left with the bushy beard is Marco. Next to him is our resident vampire look-alike, Dominic. Craven is next to him with the shaven head. Guys, this is Rowan. Be nice or I'll crack some heads open."

"Did you have a bit of trouble tonight, Shadow," Marco asked, eyeing Rowan's leg.

"Old injury," Rowan said quickly.

"Yeah, seems that buddy system I set up to keep Rowan protected didn't last six months." Shadow still couldn't believe people he trusted, who were friends of his mate, had changed their loyalty so quickly. "But the asshole's taken care of, along with four of his friends. Have you had any trouble around here while I've been out?"

"Nothing so far," Dominic said. "But people know we're here. I imagine they're waiting to see what happened with your brother. The house is in a hell of a state, but we've managed to clean out rooms for all of us, plus the living room and kitchen."

"There're plenty of people in the pack who'd be willing to work in the house for a reduction in the weekly tithe they have to pay the alpha," Rowan offered quietly. "If that was something you were thinking about, of course."

"I welcome the advice." Shadow was serious. "I've been away too long and too much has changed. Let's get inside. The pack's had enough gossip fodder for the night. I'm sure there will be more to come after the pack meeting."

"You mentioned dealing with the asshole and his friends," Marco said as they all headed inside. "Did you need for me and Craven to go and pick them up?"

"It's tempting to leave them where they fell." Shadow eased Rowan's jacket from his slim shoulders and hung it on the hook inside the door. "But yes, it's probably a good idea. Don't want kids coming across them in the morning. They are over at the entrance to Rogue Alley. Follow your nose. They stink, so you can't miss them."

"Oh wonderful," Craven groused. "Nothing like the smell of dead bodies to enhance an evening. I'd rather have latrine duty."

"You can do that tomorrow. Now git." Shadow laughed as his two friends left, muttering and grumbling all the way.

"We would have set up the master suite for you and your young mate," Dominic said, leading the way to the kitchen. "But frankly, it's a mess in there. We pulled out bags of drugs, more booze bottles than you can count, and the sheets were ready to walk out on their own. You're going to want to bin everything in there and start again. The set of rooms next to it were smaller, but they didn't look like anyone had been in there for a while and we've cleaned and set the place up with fresh linens and towels."

"Those would have been my mother's rooms. I take it the pack hasn't had an alpha female for a while?"

"Every unmated female over the age of sixteen has fancied herself as alpha female at one time or another," Rowan said. "They only lasted a week at most before Percy tossed them out on their ear. He didn't like the idea of anyone ruling the pack with him."

"What the hell happened to the morals in this place?" Shadow roared. "Drugs, booze, revolving bedroom doors. It never used to be like this."

"Ten years is a long time." To Shadow's shock, Rowan yelled back. "You've been away and have no idea what it's been like. You can't blame any of those women taking the scraps of attention they were offered. Being with Percy meant they got food, gifts they could sell and a remote chance at increasing their rank in the pack. They all knew it was a long shot. Percy's reputation is a standing joke in this place, but no one dared to mention it. But if you were hungry and couldn't afford shoes in winter, wouldn't you want to do whatever you could to get out of the poverty trap for five minutes?"

"I'm sorry. I'm just frustrated." Shadow pulled out a kitchen chair for his young mate and took the coffee Dominic offered, making sure Rowan had one too. "Everywhere I look there's something that needs fixing. I hadn't realized things had gotten so bad."

Rowan laid a hand on his arm and Shadow's skin tingled. "Once the pack sees you're genuinely trying to help them, they will pitch in and help too. Many of them are just as frustrated as you are."

"Why didn't people leave if things are so bad?" Dominic was leaning his lanky frame on the kitchen counter.

"They couldn't afford to." Rowan played with the handle on his cup. "Mr. Bell, two blocks over is a classic example. He works two jobs; his wife works as well while their five kids are at school. Instead of paying the standard twenty percent tithe to the pack, Percy decided every family had to pay in accordance with the drain they were on pack resources."

"I'm still trying to find any resources the pack is offering."

"You're sitting in it." Rowan scowled. "Percy claimed the alpha family standards needed to be maintained so every cent went into this house."

"Where?" Shadow looked around the kitchen. Most of the appliances he remembered from when he was a child. "Doesn't matter, go on. You were explaining about Mr. Bell's tithe."

"Right. Percy decided that instead of a twenty percent tithe per family, every person had to pay twenty percent of the household income."

"Er, math wasn't my strong point, but to my reckoning that means a family like Mr. Bell's would have to pay a hundred and forty percent of their income. That's impossible." Dominic scowled.

"Which is why Mr. Bell works two jobs and his wife works as well," Rowan explained. "Mrs. Bell pays sixty percent of the income she makes from her job towards the pack, which is the twenty percent for her and two of their children. Mr. Bell pays eighty percent of the income on his first job to pay for himself and the other three kids. They effectively live on the money from Mr. Bell's second job – something Percy wasn't aware he was doing otherwise he would have found a way to take a tithe on that too. A lot of the families here are living like that, and with kids, they don't have a chance to save the money to leave."

"He was robbing the pack blind." Shadow shook his head. "Why didn't anyone do anything?"

"What could they do? You're assuming there was anyone here not half dead from over work and half starved. And face it, it wasn't as though Percy ever played fair. If anyone complained or tried to see the alpha, Percy's heavies paid the family a visit and believe me, they weren't there for tea and cake. The police have been in Percy's back pocket from the start. No one has any money to get out. The best you can hope for in this pack is to not be noticed."

"How did you get on, young Rowan?" Dominic asked. "You have your own car, and your clothes are decent enough. I take it you have a job."

"I work for myself." Shadow found himself fascinated by Rowan's blush. "My grandmother used my grandfather's insurance money to send me to college. I got a degree and started creating computer games. I've recently sold one, but I haven't been paid for it yet. I imagine that's why Percy cornered me this evening. He'd be wanting a hefty chunk of the money when it came in. So far, I've been able to prove I've been living on royalty payments from other games I've helped with and as I live alone, I pay twenty percent of that."

"Pretty and smart," Dominic nodded his approval.

"And he has a deadly aim with a bag of flour and a half a dozen eggs," Shadow laughed. "My brother and his friends looked like extras in a zombie flick when I got hold of them."

"Shit, those things were for my grandmother." Rowan smacked his forehead. "How could I have forgotten? She'll need them for her baking tomorrow. She'll be so upset if she can't put something out for the kids."

Putting his cup on the counter, Dominic stretched to his full height. "I've got your gran's address. I'll go and place some orders. She'll have all she needs sitting on her doorstep in the morning." Shadow noticed his yawn was decidedly fake. "I don't know about you guys, but I'm bushed. We've worked our asses off today and I can't see things getting any easier for a while. Nice to meet you Rowan. Have a good night." With a wink and a wave, Dominic left.

Chapter Five

For a long moment, all Shadow could hear was the rumbling hum of the old refrigerator and Rowan's breathing. His mate seemed fascinated by the scratches and marks on the huge wooden table, so Shadow was surprised when he spoke.

"When I was fourteen, I had the biggest crush on you." The red on Rowan's cheeks deepened. "When you left, with nothing more than a hand in my hair, I honestly thought my heart was broken. I spent six months hoping and praying you'd realize you missed me and would come back. Of course, I was still a kid. I still believed in a happy ever after back then."

"I didn't want to get on the bus that day," Shadow admitted quietly, rubbing his chest as he remembered the pain he'd felt in it back then, increasing with every step he'd taken as he walked away from the boy he knew was destined to be his mate. "There hasn't been a day in ten years when I haven't thought of you."

"Why didn't you write, visit, something? You knew we were mates all this time. My parents were killed six months after you left. It would have meant the world to me to know I had someone on my side apart from my grandmother, especially once the pack realized I was nothing more than an omega wolf." There wasn't one ounce of condemnation on Rowan's face. He genuinely wanted to know.

Reaching over, Shadow took Rowan's hand and held it between his. "I was scared you'd ask me to come back," he said softly. "I wouldn't have been able to refuse you anything. But I couldn't come back then. I didn't trust my control. Even when you were fourteen, I used to lust after you and that just makes me a king sized perv. I remember me and the guys celebrated your eighteenth birthday in the middle of a desert. All I could think was, I could come back and claim you as mine. But when I wrote to your grandmother to ask about it, she said you were at college and asked me to wait just a bit longer.

She knew, if I came back then, you'd never be able to focus on your degree."

"She was probably right."

"We'll never know." Shadow sighed. "I signed up for another four years, which became six, all the while, waiting for the okay from your grandmother. She didn't get in touch very often, but she sent me a picture of your graduation. By then I was overseas and couldn't just leave, and well, I'm here now."

"Yep. You're here now."

Shadow waited, hoping Rowan would say more, but when he didn't, he realized his mate was waiting for him to make a move. Clearing his throat, which suddenly seemed to have a frog in it, he said softly, "I guess the question of the hour, is will you come upstairs with me now, so I can claim the mate I've waited so long for, or do you need more time to come to terms with me and what being my mate will mean?"

Peering up at him from his mass of red curls, Rowan grinned. "If I'm not claimed within the hour, you'll find your boots filled with butter, milk and anything else I can lay my hands on. I'm pretty good at using bakery goods as weapons you know."

Relief. Shadow felt incredible relief as the band around his heart finally loosened. His arousal roared like an out of control fire, unlike anything he'd experienced before. Unable to wait any longer, Shadow plucked Rowan out of his chair and into his arms. "I've waited so freaking long for this," he whispered as he leaned in for his first taste of Rowan's lips.

/~/~/~/~/

The sum total of Rowan's sexual experience was one fumbling mutual masturbation session with a fellow geek, Clarence who'd got drunk and shoved his hand down Rowan's pants while studying for their final exams. It'd been fumbling, messy and fortunately, Clarence claimed he didn't remember any of it the next day.

Shadow's kiss alone was enough to set his cock erupting with nary a touch. His mate had experience; that much was evident from the confident way Shadow's hand threaded through his curls, tilting his head just enough so their noses didn't clash. Shadow's lips were hard, just like the man himself, but he knew how to move them – sucking Rowan's bottom lip, nibbling his top lip. Feasting on his mouth like a starving man.

As Shadow stood, Rowan wrapped his legs as best he could around the man's hips, refusing to let go. Not that Shadow was showing signs of dropping him anytime soon. Already Shadow's free hand had worked its way under Rowan's shirt and Rowan shivered at the sensation of being touched. Apart from hugs from his grandmother, the only other time someone touched him in years was to hit him. This was nothing like that.

Tingles; all over tingles. When Rowan imagined his first sexual experience, he expected his cock to get hard and maybe his balls might be sensitive, but he never dreamed the term being aroused could apply to his whole body. Shadow was stroking his back as though he couldn't get enough of the feel of his skin and Rowan was fully on board. He couldn't get enough of Shadow touching him.

The slam of a door was the only clue Rowan got that they'd arrived at their destination. All of a sudden, everything felt so real and rather than be scared, Rowan realized he'd been waiting for this moment his whole life, or at least since he was fourteen.

Shadow pulled his mouth away. "I hope you're not too attached to your clothes."

"Are you?" Rowan would question where his bravado came from later. For now, he wanted to know - he was desperate to know if Shadow's body lived up to the advertising. The mattress was soft under his butt as Shadow carefully set him down, and although there was a lingering hint of dust in the air, the bed linen was clean.

But it was Shadow's scent that filled Rowan's nostrils and sent his body into overdrive. His whole life, all Rowan knew about being an omega was that it meant he could be picked on by anyone bigger than him – which was everybody. But here, in the silence of the room with his alpha looming over him as Shadow hurriedly got out of his clothes, Rowan finally appreciated his heritage.

Shadow's heaving chest was his doing. The giant bulge tenting the alpha's pants, was because of him. The flared nostrils, the rip in Shadow's shirt, was all because his alpha wanted him. By the time Shadow was naked, Rowan was transfixed by the wealth of muscles he'd never known possible on a human frame. He was so out of it, he didn't realize what Shadow was doing until he heard another rip of cloth. His shirt. And before Rowan could react, his pants were torn down the crotch and pulled gently down his legs.

"I promise I'll do my best to be gentle," Shadow said, but it was as though he was growling his words. Still lost in thinking about how long it would take to lick a mountain of muscles, Rowan didn't notice he was being flipped until his face hit the mattress.

"Ouch."

"Sorry. Hold yourself up."

Up? Up where? How? But it didn't seem Shadow was going to give him any answers. Rowan's butt was hoisted into the air and before he could say anything his butt cheeks were pulled apart. A warm, wet sensation moved over his hole and Rowan cried out. When a rumbling growl came from behind him, Rowan realized, to his shock, the licking over his most private place was intentional.

Is this what people mean by foreplay? While he spent most of his waking hours online, Rowan didn't watch porn. He knew the basics of omega anatomy, and he understood that sex for him meant he was going to get a cock in his ass, but he didn't have a clue how couples got to that point. It wasn't something he'd thought about much, and when he had, he was sure no tongue was involved.

Not that it didn't feel good. In fact, it felt really good. And the way Shadow was moaning and slurping suggested, to Rowan's innocent brain at least, that the man was enjoying himself. He kinda wished, when his brain could string a coherent thought together, that maybe he'd have had more of Shadow's kisses; maybe a chance to do some exploring of his own. But his thoughts scattered completely when he felt a blunt object pressing on his hole. Although he'd never been in his current situation before, Rowan was pretty sure that blunt object was Shadow's cock. It was far too big for a finger.

"So wet for me." Shadow was still growling. Rowan was focusing on trying to breathe as the pressure on his ass grew. "Waited so long."

Shit. This is it. Rowan was panting hard. The stretch in his muscles was so intense he was sure his ass would split in two. *How big is he?* His head down, Rowan panted, then panted some more. He was still panting when Shadow groaned, "I knew you'd be the perfect fit for me," and he felt the slap of skin against his ass cheeks.

Yeah, well maybe there were things we should've talked about before this happened. Like, how I've never done this before. Rowan wasn't sure what came next. Shadow wasn't pushing in him anymore, which was a relief, because his poor muscles could finally relax. His cock had drooped despite Shadow's intoxicating scent and his arousal earlier. The knee of his bad leg was starting to ache.

"Ready, babe?"

Rowan just nodded. With his arousal at an all-time low, he was starting to think sex wasn't all it was cracked up to be. He felt a drag against his insides. Shadow was moving. *He's pulling out. Is that it?* Rowan's whole body jolted as Shadow slammed back into him again. *I guess not.*

All Rowan could do was hang on for the ride. He'd heard others using that expression but now he finally knew what it meant. It was like being on a bucking horse, except instead of his butt slapping down on the horse's back, he was being pummeled on the inside. Shadow was moaning and grunting with every slap, mumbling terms like "so good" and "oh my gods." Rowan was just doing his best to stop from hitting his nose on the mattress.

Shadow changed positions slightly, and Rowan jolted as something foreign bloomed on his insides. It was like a spark of electricity, and to his surprise his cock started to firm up again. *This isn't so bad,* he thought as he arched his back, trying to get more of the sensation.

But he didn't get a chance to build on those feelings. Without warning, Shadow's bulk dropped over him as he slammed into Rowan's body hard. Teeth pierced the sensitive skin on Rowan's neck, and he screamed as he felt their bond snap together. It seemed only seconds later, Rowan felt Shadow withdraw his teeth, licking once over the wound Rowan knew would scar.

"So good," Shadow mumbled. "Mine now." He toppled over to the side taking Rowan with him, his cock still wedged in Rowan's ass. Within seconds he was snoring.

Rowan looked down at the mess on the covers. He'd climaxed, an automatic reflex so he'd been told that happened anytime a true mate was bitten. But there was a hollow feeling in his heart. He wiggled his hips, just a bit, and grimaced as Shadow's softening cock squelched and plopped out of him. He felt sticky and just a tiny bit used.

Shadow's arm around him was solid and heavy. Rowan debated for all of two seconds before moving it from around his waist. The bigger man didn't even stir. Scuttling across the bed, Rowan turned to look at the man who'd claimed him. In sleep, there were shades of the Gray he remembered around his eyes, the long straight nose, and the tight lips. The hard look Shadow had given Percy was gone, leaving a handsome man who'd seen a hard life.

Despite his feelings about sex, Rowan felt a fissure of hope. He had loved Gray for so long, and so desperately... *And now he's mine.* Praying the sex side of things would get better over time, Rowan got off the bed and went in search of a bathroom. No one had ever told him how messy sex could be.

Chapter Six

Shadow was instantly awake, his brain automatically assessing where he was. The ceilings above him were in need of a fresh coat of paint, but the bed was soft. The chinks of light around the drawn curtains indicated it was daylight. But it was the smell of sex in the air that really jolted his memory.

"Little red," he murmured, rolling over expecting to see his mate asleep beside him. But the bed was empty, and a quick scan of the floor showed Rowan's scattered clothes were gone. *He's probably downstairs having breakfast,* Shadow thought, leaping out of bed and heading for the bathroom. *I bet he worked up an appetite after last night.*

Or had he? As Shadow did all he needed to do, including a quick shave, he started to feel uneasy as his actions from the night before replayed in his head. His wolf was letting him know Rowan wasn't in the house, and there was a dull ache in his gut. Worse was the knowledge

Shadow might not have been the sweet and caring lover he should have been for Rowan's first time.

His suspicions were confirmed when he was greeted with three accusing faces around the kitchen table. He took the nearest seat, eyeing his friends warily.

"Rowan said he had to go back to his apartment. Something about some work he had to do," Marco said, slamming a cup of coffee on the table in front of Shadow.

"What did you do to him?" Craven said, sounding just as pissed. "The poor little guy slunk out of here like someone had kicked his dog, limping as if he'd been beaten. You had to know it was his first time. Tell me you went gently with him at least."

Limping? Oh, my gods his poor leg. I didn't even think of that. "I fucked up, guys." Shadow ran his fingers through his hair. "Ten years I've waited, knowing he was my mate. Ten fucking long years."

"That didn't stop you fucking anything that moved in the meantime," Dominic reminded harshly. "It's not as though you were celibate, even knowing you had an unclaimed mate back home. I bet Rowan didn't behave like that. Even if he didn't know he was yours, that guy has never been within spitting distance of another man's dick until last night, I'd stake my pension on it."

Shadow knew Dominic was right. Rowan's innocence showed from their first and only kiss. "He was a kid when I left. A beautiful gangly boy, with the face of an angel and a body I could not touch!" Shadow slammed his fist on the table. "You know how much it gutted me, walking away but I had no choice."

"And no one blames you for fucking your way through the ranks while you were apart," Dominic said quickly. "Alpha wolf and all those natural urges. Understandable. But that's the point. You've had close to fifteen years' worth of experience, meaning Rowan's first time should've been out of this world, the way claiming sex is supposed to be. Was it? I'm figuring it wasn't or he would have hung around for more."

Shadow thought back. He remembered the kiss that scorched his soul. He remembered ripping Rowan's clothes off that gorgeous frame and flipping the man over. "It was his ass," he said, shaking his head. "Rowan has the most delectable heart shaped ass I have ever seen. He has a light dusting of freckles, right there." He ran his hands through the air, remembering how they dusted Rowan's lower back.

Then he remembered what followed. "I behaved like a fucking cave man," he said bitterly, picking up his coffee mug and cradling it in his hands. "I forgot about Rowan's bad leg, I forgot he was a virgin and possibly didn't even know what was going on. I got a taste of his slick, my wolf surged, and I just plowed in and staked my claim. Did I tell you he has the most perfect ass I've ever seen?"

"You mentioned it," Marco said drily. "But okay, so the claiming might have been a bit harsh, but Rowan's a wolf shifter, and he's bound to have seen porn before. He works on a computer, right? But what happened afterward? You know, when he was lying in your arms looking at you with utter adoration, just like you've always dreamed? Lots of lovey-dovey kissing and cuddling, right?"

Shadow took a sip of his coffee. Then another one. He looked around the table at three of his closest friends, men who'd had his back through thick and thin, and who knew absolutely everything about him. "I rolled to one side and fell asleep. It'd been a long day, what with traveling, finding my father in that state, and then killing my brother and his friends." He shrugged. "I guess the day's events caught up with me."

His three friends groaned in unison. "Oh, fuck, Shadow," Craven said, shaking his head. "You have got some major sucking up to do. You'll be lucky if Rowan lets you anywhere near his perfect globes again. You totally ruined it. His first time, his claiming sex, and you treated him like a back alley hook up."

"Yeah, but he wouldn't know what that was like," Shadow said quickly. "It's not as though he's had back alley hook ups."

"He lives on the fringes of a wolf pack," Dominic pointed out. "He's bound to have seen it."

"And you'd better hope he doesn't think what happened last night was normal," Marco added. "Or he's going to be making excuses not to be naked with you any time soon."

"That's a thought," Shadow blinked and took another sip of his coffee, his mind working overtime. "What was Rowan wearing when he left? His shirt and pants wouldn't have covered much after I'd finished with them."

"That would explain the bundle under his arm," Craven smacked Marco on the shoulder. "Told you he wasn't stealing anything. He was wearing dirty gray sweats. I assume he got them from the clothes boxes scattered around this place."

"You thought my mate would steal from me?" Shadow fixed Marco with a glare.

"I was joking," Marco said shaking his head. "The guy looked like the slightest scare would spook him. I asked him what he'd found worth stealing seeing as he was sneaking out of here in such a hurry, and he took off. I didn't mean to upset him."

"Fucking brilliant. I'll be lucky if he even talks to me again, let alone anything else." Standing, Shadow took his cup to the bench and left it there. His gut rumbled, reminding him his last meal was lunch the day before, but he wasn't about to stop for breakfast. He had a mate to find and apologize too.

/~/~/~/~/

Rowan jumped as his computer pinged, letting him know he had a message. It'd been three hours since he'd snuck out of the alpha's house, and while he'd showered and was a lot more comfortable in his own clothes, his gut kept churning and it wasn't because of food. He had a strong feeling his mate was upset with him. Looking away from the lines of code that weren't doing a lot to keep his attention, he clicked on the chat box.

I messaged you last night. Did you finally get laid? It was Cassie, one of his best friends from university, a human with a personality as bright as her yellow blond hair. Scrolling up, he saw Cassie had indeed messaged him four times.

I had a late night, Rowan typed back quickly. His fingers hesitated above the keys. *Met someone but...*

He watched as the dots and bubble indicated Cassie was typing.

OMG, OMG, OMG. Who? Where? Tell me he's drop dead gorgeous and h-u-n-g.

Despite his upset, Rowan grinned. Cassie had no filter. Before he could stop himself, he typed, *I guess he was, seeing as my ass aches this morning. I didn't get to see his dick to be honest.*

The face palm emoji showed up, and the bubbles and dots to show Cassie was typing again. *You promised* followed by a sad face emoji. The words sounded accusing on the screen, which was ridiculous, because they were just words, but Rowan knew what Cassie was talking about. When Cassie learned he was still a virgin, which was one of those things that just came out when he was half-drunk on sherry, she made him promise he wouldn't give his "gift" as she called it to just anyone.

I didn't give my v-card to a random stranger, he typed back. *Remember me telling you about Gray?*

The stud muffin you were crushing on as a teenager? Did he come back home finally?

Yep. Rowan thought for a moment. It wasn't as though he could describe mates to a human. *It turns out he thought a lot about me while he was away.*

There was a pause, and then the bubble dot thing started up again. Rowan could imagine his friend typing madly.

Ro, you know a guy will say anything to get into your pants, right? Remember Clay who claimed he loved me to the moon and back?

Rowan remembered the nights sitting and listening to Cassie crying, while eating copious amounts of ice cream. A broken condom threw a pregnancy scare into the mix, and it was ages before his friend dated again.

Gray isn't like that, he typed even though he knew how lame that line was, at least to humans. *And besides, Clay was training to be an astronaut, so who knows, he might come back once he's been to the moon.*

Yeah, yeah, and I'll be old and gray with a dozen grandkids around my ankles by then. The bubble/dots continued after she'd hit send. *Don't think I don't know what you're doing. You are not distracting me with HIM. Did lover boy live up to expectations?*

For a moment, Rowan wished he was back at college, sitting in Cassie's messy dorm room, holding her hand and eating ice cream. *Not exactly,* he typed back. *It was a bit...* Rowan stopped for a moment, stumped for a good word. *Mechanical,* he typed finally. Then, because Cassie was his best friend, and far more experienced in sexual matters than he was, he added another line. *Is it always like that?*

As Rowan watched Cassie typing, he thought back to the morning. It was strange how his hopes the night before didn't hold up when hit with sunlight. He woke up with Shadow's chest plastered against his back and it took some maneuvering to get out of the man's octopus grasp so he could use the bathroom.

It was as he was sitting on the loo, Rowan realized Shadow hadn't been the most considerate of lover. He remembered reading a book a few weeks before where a big strong alpha had taken his little omega gently, worshipping his body and bringing him to screams of ecstasy. While he didn't expect his mating to be like the books described, his encounter with Shadow was reminiscent of sex between guys who weren't even sure if they liked each other. Ripped clothes and a punishing rhythm were more descriptive of angry sex, than the loving actions of a man intent on making his claim.

I probably read too much, Rowan thought sadly, remembering how Marco had teased him when he left. Rowan had wished he could have sunk through the floor in embarrassment when he saw the three men heading to the kitchen on his way out. His computer pinged to let him know Cassie had finally finished her message.

I know you still have deep feelings for this guy even though it's been ten years since you saw him last, Rowan read, *And I don't blame you one bit for giving up your v-card for him, especially if he's as hunky as you used to describe. But not all men are looking for their HEA, you know? So, don't go thinking bad thoughts if you don't hear from him again. And from what I've read, first time anal sex hurts big time and it can take a while for people to get used to it. It's all about perspective. It was your first time. Maybe you're actually a top?* The message was followed with a dozen smiley faces.

Hahahahaha. Rowan typed back. *We both know I'm not built that way.* And Cassie had no idea how not built for topping he was. His omega nature made him cringe at the very thought and that was without throwing Shadow's alpha nature into the mix. *I'm sure I'll see him later, maybe we can talk about it then. Him and me, I mean.*

Yeah, well if he shows up, and if you find a man who'll actually talk about that sort of stuff, he's a keeper.

You have no idea how right you are, Rowan thought as he made his excuses and said goodbye. Slumping back in his chair, he thought about what Cassie had said about perspective. *Maybe I am looking at this the wrong way.* Grabbing a piece of paper and a pen from the drawer in his desk, Rowan started to write.

1. Shadow/Gray is my fated mate.
2. He's known about me for the whole ten years he's been away.
3. He's an alpha wolf with a strong sex drive.
4. He really wanted me last night.

Rowan considered his list for a moment, then drew a line down the middle of the page and started writing on the other side.

1. Prep (lube not needed due to omega slick, but don't people stretch you with fingers first?)

Rowan didn't think a tongue counted as an ass stretching tool, although he thought he might have to research that.

2. Kissing – foreplay? Do alphas do that?
3. Going slower?
4. Could I...

A loud knock at the door stopped Rowan's train of thought. Throwing down his pen, Rowan walked to the door, his nose sniffing wildly. As soon as he caught a whiff of Shadow's unique scent, he quickly disengaged the locks on his door and threw it open. Just seeing Shadow standing there looking as delicious as he did the day before, made Rowan feel small and shy. "Hi?" He said, as his cheeks heated.

"Don't leave our bed again without telling me." Shadow pushed past the door and strode inside. Rowan barely had time to shut it before his feet left the floor and his face was smushed against Shadow's chest, a hot hand gripping his ass.

Is it possible he missed me? Rowan wondered as his lips were taken in a fierce kiss.

Chapter Seven

As far as Shadow was concerned, it'd taken him far too long to get to Rowan's grandmother's, secure Rowan's address and make his way to his mate's small apartment. Rowan's grandmother's eyes held the same twinkle they always had, even as he muttered something along the lines that he might have fucked up. She made him sit down and eat two of the muffins she placed in front of him, under the guise of searching for Rowan's address. Considering she eventually pulled it out from under an old phone book sitting on the kitchen counter, Shadow knew it didn't have to take that long.

While he'd eaten, she chatted generally, although as he was driving to Rowan's he realized she'd made some good points about the pack. The children, who all scattered when he strode away from Grandma's house, did look thin and wary, something he'd only seen in war zones. He didn't see any adults, although he was aware of eyes peering at him from out of the houses as he went to his car. *Hopefully the pack meeting will help,* he thought as he drove away.

But now, he was in Rowan's apartment and the man was in his arms. All Shadow wanted to do was throw him down and sink deep into his body just as he had the night before. If he hadn't picked up Rowan's wince as he cupped the ass he was coming to adore, infinitesimal to the naked eye, he might well have done it. But instead he pulled back on his wolf and his urges, and took Rowan over to a small couch, settling his mate on his lap. He was not going to think about how delicious the pressure on his cock was from Rowan's hip.

"You have a nice apartment," he said, looking around. It was small; tiny in comparison to the mansion he'd grown up in when he was still known as Gray, and the house he knew Rowan lived with his parents when he was a kid. There was no dining table – just a large desk set up with three computer screens, one of which seemed to be rolling lines of code over the wide screen. A battered computer chair looked more worn than the couch they were sitting on, and the tiny kitchenette was clean and looked barely used.

"It was what I could afford." Rowan shrugged, ducking his head.

The smell of his arousal lingered in the air, testing Shadow's control. Unused to flowery speeches or having to discuss feelings, Shadow decided to be blunt. "Did I hurt you last night?" He rested his free hand over Rowan's twisting fingers.

Rowan wouldn't look at him and that wasn't a good sign. "It's not like I have anything to compare it to." He nibbled on his bottom lip. "Is it always like that?"

"You mean am I always a callous uncaring lover, who didn't give a shit whether you came or got any pleasure out of what we were doing at all?" Shadow's laugh wasn't a happy one. "You could say that's what I've been used to since I was away, but you deserved a lot better for your first time."

Rowan flinched again, noticeable this time. Shadow wanted to slap himself around the head. "I'm sorry. I should never have mentioned anyone else. They meant nothing and were merely a willing hole in the dark when I was lonely."

Rowan didn't say anything, but he seemed to find the ends of his fingernails really interesting. Shadow bit back his frustration. Gently tilting Rowan's face up, he said quietly, "things are not going to be easy between us if you don't talk to me."

"I don't know what you want me to say," Rowan said simply, and Shadow was pleased to see he had no problem meeting his eyes. "The knee on my bad leg ached in that... in that position... and I wasn't sure what you were actually doing until you did it. I would've liked more kisses or something first, but then I was talking to my friend and she mentioned perception, and I wondered if maybe I've just read too many romance books and that maybe the way you did it was just the way it was for everyone."

Well, shit damn and fucking hell. Shadow gave himself a mental whack around the head that time. "Little red, I promise, you deserve so much better than what I gave you last night." He cleared his throat. Talking like this was hard. "I was a bad, bad, wolf, and I'm not going to hide that or make excuses for it. Yes, it'd been a rough day, and yes, I've waited ten years to hold you in my arms..."

"Sounds like you're making those excuses anyway." To Shadow's relief, Rowan was grinning.

"You're right." Shadow allowed his own smile to shine through. "There is no excuse. I'm just really sorry that I ruined your first time, because that is something you'll never get back."

"It wasn't ruined exactly." Rowan inhaled sharply. "I mean, I came and everything, which I guess was supposed to happen when you bit me, and I know I belong to you now, but..."

"But what, little red?" Shadow ran his fingers through Rowan's curls. They were so soft.

"I felt a bit," Rowan's fingers made circular movements above his heart, "sort of hollow inside afterward. Does that make sense?"

Letting out a long sigh, Shadow nodded. He knew that feeling all right. It was exactly the same way he felt every time he zipped up after fucking someone who wasn't his mate. He'd tried so hard, after Rowan turned eighteen, even though he was miles away to stay true to his mate. But his natural high sex drive meant he had slip ups, and that hollow feeling he experienced afterward got more intense every time. "I am so sorry, my sweet mate. I understand completely. Things will get better; I promise and if there's something you'd like to try…"

"Really?" Rowan's eyes widened. "Only, after chatting with Cassie, and thinking about perception and everything, I made a list. Did you want to see?"

A list? All Shadow could do was nod as Rowan leaped off his lap and headed over to the desk. From what he read between the lines of what Rowan had said before, his mate hadn't been an avid porn watcher, so hopefully nothing on the list was too kinky. Shadow liked sex, good hard sex. He didn't have the time or inclination to play the games some people enjoyed.

Taking the paper Rowan handed to him, Shadow scanned it quickly. "Well," he said, mentally relieved there was nothing offensive on the paper. "You were right about the four things listed on the left side of the paper. I am your mate, I am an alpha, I do have a high sex drive like all alphas do, and I really, really wanted you last night."

Rowan leaned to one side to see it for himself. "Oh, that was me putting things into perspective." He leaned away again, rocking on the balls of his feet.

"Okay, so the right-hand side of the paper is the things you were hoping for, right?" Shadow read the list, biting the inside of his lip. *Those are all the things I promised myself I would do, and didn't,* he thought, miffed his sweet omega mate actually missed out because he was being a Neanderthal.

Clearly, he'd been quiet too long, because Rowan said nervously, "you arrived before I got it finished, and it's not as though anything on there is really important, or anything. It was just the sort of things I thought I might like…"

"The list is fine. More than fine. It's you expressing the things you hope for when you think of your time with me." Shadow looked up and held out his hand. When Rowan took it, he tugged the man gently onto his lap. "You are right about the prep. It was your first time, and while omegas don't usually need a lot of prep as a rule, I should have been more considerate."

"Been with a lot of omegas, have you?" Rowan shot him a sideways glare.

"You're my first and only," Shadow said quickly. "Kissing, foreplay; yes, alphas do that, or at least that is what I hoped to do with you, and that is what I will do from now on, and the same with going slower. I can't promise it will be like that all the time..."

"Because sometimes you just want to jump my bones?"

"Exactly. Hopefully, when we're more used to each other, you won't mind it either." Shadow loved Rowan's little smirk. He pointed to number four, which was unfinished. "What were you hoping you could do?" *He's my mate. If he wants to top me, I'll take it. Maybe.*

Rowan's cheeks were bright red. "I wanted to be able to touch you," he said, hesitantly resting his hand on Shadow's chest. "You're so big, and you're built like a mountain. I wanted to be able to explore what makes you happy sometimes, maybe, if you'd let me, or didn't mind..."

"I really stuffed things up by falling asleep as soon as the spunk dried, didn't I?" Shadow said with a small smirk.

"Before the spunk dried, you mean." Rowan's smirk was bigger. "I was a mess with goo covering me front and back. No one ever mentions that in the books I read."

Shadow groaned and physically slapped his head this time. "What I should've done, when we were finished, was ease myself gently from your body and go and get a damp washcloth to clean us both up. Then, I should have cuddled you close, and we'd have talked about all sorts of things like how we hope our future together is going to grow, and then we'd have had sex again, and probably another couple of times before the night was over and then after we'd finally gotten a few hours sleep, we would have stumbled downstairs and ignored my friends teasing us as I cooked you a huge breakfast."

"The breakfast would have been nice," Rowan said, rubbing his belly.

Shadow dithered for all of two seconds. The apartment was small, but private. He could have a second go at making Rowan's body dance with pleasure under his touch, or... Standing up, he set Rowan on his feet and took his hand. "What's good around here?" He asked, leading his mate to the door. "It's been ten years since I've been around, remember. Is Barney's still the same as it used to be? They used to cook the most amazing steaks."

"They have steaks." Rowan nodded. He waved his hand in the direction of Shadow's crotch. "But didn't you want to, you know, first?"

"You will notice, after you've been around me for a while, that I will always 'want to you know' when I'm around you," Shadow said sincerely. "Always. No question. Any time of the day or night. But there are other things in life, like eating, and taking a shower, and going out once in a while."

"And looking after the pack," Rowan reminded him as he grabbed his keys from the table by the door. "That's going to take a lot of time and energy."

Why do you think we're going to breakfast out instead of back at the pack house? Shadow wanted to cement his claim on his sweet omega a bit more, before he had to deal with any other unpleasantness.

Chapter Eight

The breakfast was fun. Rowan enjoyed listening to Shadow talk about his life in the military, and he preened under the interest his mate showed in his work. It was the first time Rowan had ever been on a date as such and watching how Shadow's face lit up when he laughed telling stories about his friends was almost enough to distract him from the delicious full steak breakfast they'd both ordered. In that moment, it was easy to forget they were part of a troubled pack. They could be just two men who had nothing to think about but themselves and their own little corner of the world.

It didn't last. Rowan had just unlocked the door to his apartment, Shadow hot and heavy at his back, gripping at his hips and rubbing against him, when Shadow's phone went off. "What, damn it?" Shadow growled into his phone as Rowan walked inside. "I told you, I'm with my mate."

Unwilling to be caught eavesdropping, which was an easy thing for a wolf shifter to do, Rowan went into his bedroom. Shadow had asked him to pack a bag for a few days. There hadn't been any decisions made on where they would live over the long term, but Shadow asked him to at least consider staying at the pack house for now.

He was just arranging his clothes in his overnight bag when Shadow came in. "No time for sex, I take it?"

"There's a group of guys at the mansion," Shadow said angrily. "They won't leave. They won't say what they want. My men can't just kick them out because they smell of pack, but they also smell of drugs and goodness knows what else."

"More of Percy's cronies." Rowan zipped up his bag and grabbed his laptop. He wasn't sure if Shadow had a computer at his house but preferred using his own anyway. "So why the long face? Are you going to insist I stay here while you go off, doing your thing?"

From the flash of guilt passing over Shadow's face, that was exactly what the man was going to say, and Rowan got his own flash – of annoyance. "I see. I'm mate in name only, am I? I'll just stay here and plod along on my computer, and you'll what? Come and see me when you want sex, is that it?"

"No, no, it's not like that." Shadow ran his hands over his face and groaned. "This confrontation isn't going to be pleasant; you have to know that. You lived with these assholes."

"Exactly." Putting down his bags, Rowan stormed over to his mate, prodding him on the chest with his finger. "I've lived with them for ten years and know more about them than you. I know their weaknesses, I know their threat level to you, me, and other innocent members of the pack. You go in there blind and you could be homeless by nightfall."

"There's no one strong enough in the pack to take me out."

Shadow seemed shocked by Rowan's anger and to be honest, so was Rowan, but he wasn't going to back down now. "I'm either your mate, and I stand by your side, or you can go and be alpha without me, completely. Understood?"

"You don't want to be with me anymore? But..."

"That's not what I said, you butt head. We're mates and no one can tear us apart. But if you aren't going to treat me like an alpha mate, and just come and see me when you want somewhere to stick your dick, or drag me back to the pack house to parade me in front of visiting alphas because you've got an omega and they haven't, you can keep your pants zipped and host your own damn dinners and pack meetings."

Rowan hated the look of worry on Shadow's face and hated more that he'd put it there. But instinct told him that if he didn't stand up for himself now, he'd be living forever in Shadow's shadow. The play on words made him grin, even if it wasn't appropriate.

"Am I alpha mate?" he asked more quietly now his point was made; flattening his hand over Shadow's heart. "Or just your part time mate?"

Shadow breathed out heavily, and covered Rowan's hand with his own. "You're mine," he said simply, but Rowan saw the devotion in Shadow's eyes as he said those two words. "We'd better get going before there's a riot at the pack house."

Rowan accepted the answer for what it was for now, staying silent as Shadow carried his bags down to the car. He waited until they were heading into pack territory before he said, "You know, you never answered my question back there."

The muscle under Shadow's jaw tightened. "It wasn't that I didn't want you with me," he said, his eyes focused on the road. "I'm just not sure if I want to be alpha, so I couldn't tell you if you're alpha mate or not."

Rowan twisted slightly in his seat so he could see Shadow more clearly. "A person is born to be an alpha, the same as I was born to be an omega. It's not possible to go against our status."

"I meant the alpha of our home pack," Shadow flashed him a quick smile before focusing on the road again. "I know it was foolish of me, but while I was away, I didn't know any of the shit that was going down back home. The only letters I got were from your grandmother, and they were about you. In my head, I used to dream of coming home, sweeping you off your feet and us heading off for parts unknown to make a new life for both of us and a few of my friends."

"You didn't know your father was sick at all?" Rowan gasped as Shadow shook his head. "So, you didn't come back to take over being alpha?"

"I came back for you and that's all," Shadow said as he turned their car into the driveway. "In my head, my father would still be ruling this place another hundred or so years. It took me five minutes after seeing my father again to see all my hopes of leaving with you go down the toilet. Mind you, if it hadn't had been for Percy, I still would have taken you and run. I could've gotten the council to appoint another alpha if the pack had been running well. My brother did a lot of damage while I was away."

"I'm so sorry, I didn't know." Rowan reached over, resting his hand over Shadow's on the gear stick. He still had questions like why did Shadow invite his friends if he'd only come to claim a mate. But those questions would have to wait. The grim faces of Marco and Craven, who were guarding the door had to be dealt with first.

Rowan gave Shadow's friends credit. They didn't blink at all seeing him get out of the car. The warmth of Shadow's hand caressed his lower back as they walked slowly up the porch stairs. Shadow flashed a hand signal at Marco who raised four fingers. "We put them in the living room," Craven whispered as they moved past. "Told them there was nowhere else suitable for now. Dominic is in your father's old office trying to make heads and tails of things in there."

A curt nod was the only sign Shadow gave to indicate he'd heard Craven's words. Rowan let himself be led through the large hall and into the family living room. He mentally shrunk back when he saw who was lounging over the alpha's furniture. If Shadow noticed his hesitation, he didn't mention it.

"Gentlemen," Shadow said sharply. "Is this any way to show respect to your new alpha?"

Gavin, a person Rowan was uncomfortably familiar with, flicked his lanky blond hair out of his dark eyes, and slowly removed his feet from the coffee table. He didn't get out of his seat. "I had to come and see for myself if it was true," he drawled. "Word's running around the pack like wildfire that good ol' Percy had an accident last night with some of his friends." His leer flashed over to Rowan making him uncomfortable.

"What happened to my brother and his friends was no accident." Rowan noticed how Gavin started at the brother reference, narrowing his eyes as he tried to connect Gray with Shadow. "If you wanted to know what happened, you could've simply waited for the pack meeting tonight like everyone else."

"Yeah, there's a bit of a problem with that." Gavin checked his friends were still hanging onto his every word and action. Two of them, Jack and Donny had their fists bunched as though itching for a fight. Talon had his hands in his pockets staring at the wall paper, probably fingering the knife Rowan knew he kept there.

"You see, Percy and us, we had a bit of an arrangement, so we'd thought we'd make ourselves available to you, get inducted into the inner circle, so to speak, before the meeting. I mean, we don't want any of the mutually beneficial arrangements we had with Percy to fall flat just because the silly bugger got himself killed, now do we?"

"What sort of mutually beneficial arrangements are you talking about?" Shadow folded his arms across his chest and Rowan was just glad he wasn't the focus of his mate's gaze in that moment. Either Gavin hadn't noticed the change in Shadow's attitude, or he was just too thick to notice.

"Well, it's lots of things, ain't it, boys?" Gavin leaned back in his seat, sharing a chuckle with his friends. "Anything you need really; we get it for you. Acquisitions, a bit of heavy work if you know what I mean. Booze, dames, something a little bit spicier, I'm sure you get my drift. You could call us the pack acquisition crew if you like."

"You supply all these things to the *pack*?" Shadow's tone hadn't changed, and Gavin grinned like an idiot.

"Well, not the pack per se, so to speak. I mean, who cares about that bunch of drones, right? But they do bring in a healthy income thanks to Percy upping the tithes and the inner circle has to get some benefits out of that. Am I right, or am I right?" He laughed loudly, slapping his leg with his hand.

"I see." Shadow inhaled sharply and the side of his lip curled up. "Mr... I'm sorry, I don't believe you introduced yourself."

"Oh, right, yeah of course." Gavin jumped to his feet and held out his hand. "Gavin Parks is the name. You probably don't remember me. I was about five years behind you at school." He waved at his friends to stand with him when Shadow made no move to shake hands with him. "This is my crew, Jack, Donny and Talon. You have to watch Talon, he's a mean bugger with the knife if you know what I mean."

"I know exactly what you mean, Mr. Parks," Shadow's voice now held a steel edge. "In fact, I've understood everything you've said so far. According to you, the pack members are nothing but drones, the inner circle apparently funnels pack money to buy your acquisitions, and you want that system to continue now I've taken over. Have I left anything out?"

Gavin looked at Donny who pointed his finger at Rowan. "You might want to get rid of the omega," Donny said in what he probably thought was a friendly tone. "Ol' Percy never let trash like him near the place. Your reputation is going to suffer if you're seen with him anywhere near you. Omega's are nothing but a walking glory hole when you think about it."

"Oh, I have thought about everything you've said," Shadow snarled. "Answer me this. How long will it take you to pack all your belongings?"

Gavin's face brightened. "Hey, we're going to move in here. Hear that guys? We've been invited to live in the alpha's mansion."

"You haven't been invited anywhere except out." Shadow's snarl intensified. "You have exactly one hour to clear out all your belongings and get out of my territory. If me or my men catch one sniff of your stench anywhere near this house or my territory, you'll be buried right alongside your old pal, Percy and his other friends. Got it?"

Gavin's mouth dropped open as his friends stared. Then his eyes narrowed, and Rowan felt them burn his skin. "It was you, wasn't it? You worthless piece of shit. You snuck up on the alpha and told him a whole bunch of lies about how things are done around here. Just because I knocked your granny down the steps one time, you've had it in for me."

"I didn't know you hurt my grandmother," Rowan cried. "If I had, I would've done this a long time ago." Without thinking about the consequences to his bad leg or anything else for that matter, Rowan sprinted over, kicking Gavin right between the legs. The man howled as he crumpled to his knees. "You bastard," Rowan screamed, kicking the man in the head this time. "That sweet old lady feeds four of your kids every day and you hit her?"

His bad leg buckled, and it was just as well, because he felt the swoosh of a fist fly past his face. "You stuck up little shit," Donny yelled as he made to punch him again. Jack was right there with him and Rowan knew he was in for a world of hurt. But he was still seeing red, the thought of his grandmother, the one genuinely sweet person in his whole world being hurt was more than he could stomach. He balled his fists and swung upwards. Maybe he'd get lucky twice. But it was Craven's open palm he hit.

"Hold up, there tiger." Craven showed his teeth. "I'm one of the good guys. Let me help you up."

"Shadow?" Rowan stumbled and used Craven's arm to steady himself. The enormity of what he'd just done hit him like a sledge hammer and he groaned. "My gods, what must he think of me now?"

"Couldn't be prouder of my alpha mate," Shadow yelled from the other side of the room. Peering around Craven, Rowan saw all four of their visitors were trussed up with zip ties. Marco was frisking Talon, pulling a half a dozen knives out of various pockets around his person. "Have you got anything to say to these idiots before they're banished for good?"

"I want restitution for my grandmother." Rowan pushed himself off Craven's arm, testing his leg. *I can do it,* he told himself firmly as he hobbled across the room. "Every single day without fail, my grandmother bakes and puts out food so the children of Rogue Alley can eat. They don't talk to her. They often spit on her or snarl if she tries to touch them, but every day, rain or shine, she provides for the smallest and weakest members of this pack. She barely stands at five foot, and she's lucky if she'd weigh a hundred pounds. And you hit her. Knocked her down as though she was nothing. What type of man does that make you?"

"One better than you," Jack decided to speak up on Gavin's behalf, lifting the side of his lip. Marco slapped the snarl right off him, but he didn't stop talking. "You slink in here like a cat in heat, throwing yourself at the first alpha you see in the hopes of getting a permanent position. You're the idiot here, not me. Everyone knows the alphas of this pack have never had an alpha mate, and in a week, maybe less after today, you're going to be out on your ear and scrabbling for scraps like the rest of us."

Shadow growled, and then said, "Show him, little red."

Show him what? But as Rowan caught the look of pride in his mate's eyes, he realized what Shadow wanted. Opening up the neck of his shirt, he pulled it aside, showing the huge scar left by Shadow's teeth. "My mate, the Alpha, came home for me," he said meeting Jack's eyes, then looking at Donny, Talon and Gavin. "He didn't want any trouble. He just wanted me. But like any decent, honorable alpha, when he saw what was happening to the people here, he decided to stay and put things right. Unlike you, who crawled in here, thinking this alpha was going to be as easy to intimidate as his beta brother. To my way of thinking this scar makes me alpha mate, and before the hour is up, you four will be rogues. I know who I'd rather be."

Craven clapped and laughed, causing Rowan to jump. He didn't realize the man was standing so close behind him. He got a warm flutter in his heart when he realized the man was there in case he fell. Marco and Shadow were laughing too, the four tied up men looking more worried by the second.

As he looked them over one last time, he saw Talon trying to catch his eye. "Before I get kicked out, can I speak to you and the alpha privately?" he whispered, casting a worried look at his friends.

Rowan looked over at Shadow who gave a barely there nod. "Talon will stay here for the moment. Marco, would you and Craven mind kicking the rest of the trash out and make sure they leave the territory within the next fifty minutes?"

"On it, Alpha Mate," Marco grinned broadly.

"Always a pleasure, Alpha Mate," Craven added.

"I'll get you. I know people who know people. I'll get you for this." Gavin was still screaming as Marco dragged him away. Rowan's body swayed, but the sight of Talon still lying where he'd been placed in his bonds kept him on his feet. Fortunately, it didn't take long for Shadow to reach his side, sliding his arm around his waist, holding him firmly, almost intimately, given the situation. Rowan allowed his body to relax. Now they just had to find out what Talon wanted. Hopefully he could sit down first.

Chapter Nine

Shadow hadn't known whether to be proud or horrified when Rowan kicked Gavin in the balls, but he was already moving to intercept when Jack and Donny went to hit his wee mate. Fortunately, Craven and Marco had been standing just outside the living room while the meeting was going on and were just as quick to lend a hand when Shadow needed them.

But gods, he wanted his mate something fierce. He didn't know until that minute how turned-on he could be by Rowan's show of spirit. Despite his omega status, Rowan was feisty and had a deeply caring nature. Which was why Shadow was escorting his now heavily limping mate to the nearest chair, instead of whisking him upstairs for some slow sensual loving.

"Thank you. That was kind of a dumb thing for me to do," Rowan said, sitting down and easing his leg out straight.

"We might have to invest in a brace for this leg, if you're going to make a habit of kicking people." Kneeling in front of Rowan's chair, Shadow ran his hand up the injured calf muscle. The muscles jumped under his hands, and they were definitely tight and felt hot to the touch. "A warm bath might be in order, I think," he said softly, looking up and catching Rowan's dazed expression. "When we've finished our duties here, of course."

"Of course." Rowan snapped his mouth shut, but his eyes blazed with a heat Shadow hoped he'd live up to very soon. Before things could get too hot and heavy between them, Shadow straightened up, looking over at Talon who seemed almost sad watching them together.

"You said you wanted to talk to me and Rowan." Shadow slid into the seat next to his mate. "Talk."

Struggling to get into a sitting position, Talon tilted his head to one side, showing his neck. "Despite Gavin's words, I am not, and never have been part of his crew. I do my best to help others where I can, but it's never done any good for anyone

116

to show any weakness around here, which is why I carry my knives. Most people don't mess with me, because they know I can use them."

Shadow wasn't sure he was convinced of the man's good intentions, although there was no scent of deceit coming off him. Talon turned his gaze to Rowan. "Alpha Mate, did your grandmother tell you I visited her, after Gavin knocked her down the steps? Did she tell you what that was about?"

Rowan shook his head. "I didn't even know she'd been hurt," he said sadly. "But then, she wouldn't tell me anyway. I know some of the older kids give her a hard time sometimes, but I thought because she offered food to anyone who asked, and even those who don't ask, that she'd be left alone. She's a pack widow. Her husband served this pack proudly, back when it was something to be proud about."

"I know what you mean," Talon said glumly, and Shadow realized Talon and Rowan were probably about the same age. "It was food that riled Gavin up that time. She'd given out some muffins to probably a dozen kids when Gavin saw her. He demanded some, made to snatch one off one of the kids, and your grandmother whacked him with her tray."

Shadow bit the inside of his lip, imagining Rowan's grandmother doing exactly that.

"The kids all scattered – you know how they are," Talon continued. "Gavin was furious, looming over her, demanding her baking, but she didn't have any left. That's when he pushed her. Someone else from down the street yelled out, telling him to stop being an ass and leave her alone and Gavin sauntered off down the road like his shit didn't stink. I... I couldn't stay... helping her would've made matters worse, but I kept an eye on her until I saw she'd made it inside."

"At least someone was looking out for her," Rowan sighed. "I asked her time and time again to come and live with me because I was worried about something like this happening, but she wants to spend her last days in the house she shared with her husband."

"She won't leave. Your grandmother loves those kids," Talon said. "And face it, up until now, those kids have needed her. But look, I did go back the next day. Your gran," Talon shook his head with a small smile. "Even though she clearly saw me with Gavin the day before, she invited me in, made me tea and gave me cake. I'd never had cake before."

Talon's voice had a wistful edge, and Shadow knew the man wasn't like his friends. Maybe Talon realized his tone was betraying too much, because he said, "I helped her all I could and believe it or not, I've helped you too in the past, Alpha Mate. You walk down Rogue Alley every freaking Friday night, and I've used numerous excuses to ensure Gavin wasn't in the area when you did. I know I didn't have to. You didn't ask me to. But that man had a hard on for you that wouldn't quit and I... I couldn't let him hurt you."

"Why?" Rowan asked quietly, and Shadow was glad he did. He wanted to know as well.

Talon sat up as straight as he could with his hands still bound behind his back. "My mom died when I was a pup. My dad ran off and I haven't seen him in a dozen or more years. My granddaddy raised me as best he could, which wasn't easy because as soon as Shadow left, Percy started making his mark on the pack. My granddaddy has been dead these past three years now, but I remember him saying, as clear as day. A wolf shifter is judged by how he treats the weakest members of the pack. You're the pack omega. You didn't deserve to be picked on or treated like dirt all the time."

Shadow's eyes narrowed. He'd been watching Talon's face, and while the boy wasn't lying, there was something more he wasn't saying. "If you want the chance to stay in this pack," he said firmly, "then I need to know you aren't going to cause any more bother, and that means you need to be open and honest with me about *everything*. Tell me the rest of the reason you didn't want to see my mate hurt."

"Geez, you'd think a guy would be grateful I looked out for his mate as best I could, especially when the likes of Beau and Saul let him down," Talon huffed. "Fine, you want to know why I didn't want to see your precious mate hurt? Because he made something of himself, okay? An omega wolf. Parents dead. You left him with no support but his granny who couldn't fight her way out of a paper bag. But despite all that, despite the shit this pack went through, Rowan still went to college. Do you know how rare that is in this pack? He was the only one. Not only did he go to college and get his degree, but he came back. He didn't have to. But he visited every weekend while he was at school, and when his degree was done, he came back, working at whatever it is he does, and making something good of himself. He's an example, Alpha, can't you see that? A positive example of what this pack could do if they're just given a chance. I didn't want to see that ruined just because Rowan was born an omega and some of the dicks around here got the wrong idea about what that meant."

"You really see me that way?" It seemed it wasn't only Shadow who was shocked by Talon's outburst. Rowan sounded almost in tears and Shadow reached over, putting his arm around his mate's shoulder.

"Ro, you and your granny are two of the sweetest people in this pack." Talon shook his head as though disgusted with himself. "Look, having heart to hearts, spilling about feelings and shit like that. It's not who I am. But I always saw you as an example of how I could do better, how this pack could do better. Most of the people here are so busy trying to keep their heads above water, they don't have a chance to think of doing better for themselves in the future."

Shadow wasn't surprised when Talon met his eyes, briefly, but the contact was made before Talon's eyes shied away. "I'll beg if I have to," Talon said quietly. "I knew as soon as I saw you Alpha, so proud with Ro by your side, that this pack can change for the better. I'd like the chance to be a part of that."

"You don't have to beg," Rowan said quickly. "Shadow's going to give you the chance, aren't you, Alpha? Talon has tried to help me in the past. I've still got one of his knives in my drawer in my apartment as proof."

"He used one of his knives on you?" Shadow knew he was growling but just the thought of one curl on Rowan's head being threatened was enough to make him want to tear something apart.

"I found the knife," Rowan said with a smile which was shared between Shadow and Talon. Talon's pale face had bright red slashes where his cheeks were. "Someone, I don't know who, was following me one night when I was on my way back to my car after visiting my grandmother. Then suddenly, I could hear scuffling, yelling, there was all sorts going on and I have to admit I ran as best as I could to get to the car. I had just started my car when I saw Saul and Beau coming out of the alley. They didn't see me, they were too busy clutching their arms, and mumbling to themselves about ninja assassins or something."

Talon laughed. Shadow glared.

"Anyhow," Rowan said, "I don't know why I did it, but I turned the car engine off, and crept back down the alley. I don't know, I worried someone was hurt. And that's when I saw the knife embedded into an old wooden box. It was shiny, had obviously been well cared for, and I was sure then it was you looking out for me Talon. I just couldn't say anything, because, well, you know…"

"The same reason I couldn't talk to you." Talon seemed weary. "It's well past time for a change. We all deserve something better."

It was Talon's last statement that pushed Shadow out of his seat. Crossing over to where Talon was sitting, Shadow reached behind the man, snapping the ties around his wrists with his bare hands, before bending over and doing the same with the ties around Talon's feet.

"You can get your second chance," Shadow said, straightening and reaching out his hand to help Talon to his feet. "But there will be none of this skulking in the dark alleys or going back to your old ways. If you want to be a true member of this renewed pack, then you have to live openly by your grandfather's words."

"I won't let you down." Talon tilted his neck and Shadow rested his hand, just briefly on the young man's neck, giving him the acceptance he asked for.

"I'm glad," Shadow said as he withdrew his hand. "Because your second chance comes with a new job. I want you to move into the pack house, unless you have someone you are caring for already?"

Talon shook his head. "There's only me, and I've been dossing on couches where I can since Percy sold my grandfather's house from under me."

More shit I have to deal with. "I'll take care of that too, but for now, you'll move in here, and when I'm not around you will be the alpha mate's shadow."

"You're getting me a bodyguard?" Rowan didn't sound very happy about the prospect.

"There's going to be big changes in this pack and not everyone is going to be happy about them. I know you have things you want to do in a day, and I don't want to stop you going out, but there will be times when I can't go with you, and that's when I want Talon with you."

"I'll do it," Talon said quickly. His grin at Rowan was open and Shadow noticed he was a good-looking guy now his scowl and attitude were gone. "I always wanted to know what you do with all your book smarts anyway. This way, I might get some ideas about what I want for my own future."

Nailed it. Shadow kept his smirk to himself. Talon probably didn't realize it, but with just a few choice words he'd stripped any argument Rowan might have had about having someone watch out for him. It was close. Rowan's mouth even opened, but then with a long sigh, he closed it again.

"I live a boring life," he said to Talon. "Or at least I did until the alpha came home. What do you know about computers?"

"Not a lot," Talon's grin widened. "But I'm keen to learn."

"That's settled then," Shadow said, reaching out his hand for his mate, to help him up this time. "Take the rest of the day to get any stuff you have together. Speak to Dominic about anything you need. Take one of the spare rooms – you'll scent which ones are taken, and you'll probably need some cleaning gear too because a lot of this house hasn't been touched by a duster in at least ten years. Report to us here, at six o'clock tonight, just before the pack meeting, and you can start then."

"I won't let you down, Alpha." Talon nodded respectfully. "You've given me this one chance and I won't blow it. You have my word."

"I'll see you at six." Shadow watched as Talon sprinted off, trusting his instincts wouldn't let him down. He knew Rowan was watching him and allowed himself a smirk. Deciding action was better than listening to his mate tell him off when they'd only been mated for less than a day, he stood, reaching down to scoop Rowan into his arms.

"Shadow..."

"Hush, little red. We're going to have that bath I promised you," Shadow strode out of the living room, Rowan safe in his arms. He saw Dominic poke his head out of his father's office, but when his friend saw the determined look on his face, he ducked away again. Yes, he was sure Dominic had a lot to say about how the pack finances and goodness knows what else he found in the office, but that could wait until after he'd seen to his mate.

Chapter Ten

"This is just obscene," Rowan said, scanning the figures on the printed sheets Dominic had given him. "Look at this. Over thirty families, contributing up to a thousand dollars every single week as pack tithe, and the money's not going anywhere to help the pack at all. Cash withdrawals, strip clubs, takeaway bars, and liquor shops." He looked up at Shadow who was looking over papers of his own. "Please tell me that's the first thing you're going to do tonight. Reduce this tithe."

"The investments my father set up years ago are paying good dividends. That means the payouts to people like your grandmother were paid despite what Percy was doing," Shadow said. "But there's also begging letters here from the school, the food program, and the elders for money for 'impoverished' pack members."

"Yeah, don't be so sure the elders want that money for anything more than a vacation," Rowan said absently. He was reading a list of rents collected by the Alpha family. In most packs, houses were included as part of the benefits that came from lending their strength and support to the alpha. But Percy had been charging rent to most families, on top of the tithe. "These rents shouldn't be charged either," he said, looking up to see Shadow with a shocked look on his face.

"I'll stop them immediately." Shadow looked at his friends then back at Rowan. "What did you mean about the elders using the money for vacation purposes?"

Rowan couldn't see what the problem was. That was one of the pack's worse kept secrets. "They each do it at least four times a year. Because of the way the pack finances are set up, the elders can request money for 'services' every quarter to allocate as they see fit to help the pack."

"That's standard in most packs. A payment was made to Elder Clinton last week for twenty thousand dollars," Craven said, handing over a bank statement.

"That's about right," Rowan glanced at the paper and handed it back. "He's not likely to be at the meeting tonight unless someone's called him to tell him what's going on. He'll be in Italy getting a tan. He goes there at least twice a year."

"But the elders are meant to ensure the alpha doesn't victimize any pack members, ensuring that everyone is treated fairly and has access to all they need." Marco looked around the office. "What am I missing here?"

"The level of corruption in this pack, maybe?" Talon said from where he was leaning on the doorframe. "I did try to explain this to you guys this afternoon. Well, not the alpha and alpha mate, obviously, because the alpha mate was getting his leg tended to." Only Talon could make that sound obscene. Rowan flushed, because his new friend wasn't wrong in his assumption. Rowan found he didn't have to worry about his bad leg at all, if Shadow stood over him in the bath and fed him his cock. "Percy was a lot of things, but stupid wasn't one of them. He knew paying off the elders would keep them quiet about anything else that he got up to in the pack."

"Corrupt elders, starving pack members, the houses are so rundown a decent wind will blow them down." Shadow huffed out a long sigh. "And I've got to get these people to trust me tonight."

"I've got a list of things that can help," Rowan said brightly, then he flushed under Shadow's searching gaze. "I didn't really need that nap you insisted on this afternoon."

"You knew about all this?" Dominic shook the handful of papers he'd been going through.

"Not the finances, no," Rowan said. "I don't think even Percy or any of his friends knew much about it either. They had a cash card, they just kept drawing on the accounts and didn't really care about the balances. If they did hit a week where their card declined, they'd just find another tax to slap on the pack, or raise the tithes, or sell another pack house."

"So, how can your list help?" Shadow asked slowly. "If you didn't know all this *shit*," he snarled, flinging his hands to show the mounds of papers Dominic had been working on, "how can you know how to get these people to trust us?"

"It's just as well I know your anger is simply frustration at the mess you've been left to deal with," Rowan said calmly. "If I thought it was directed at me, we'd be having words, Alpha."

Craven, Dominic, and Marco laughed, and even Talon covered his mouth with his hand, his eyes shining above it.

"It's simple. I've lived this and so has Talon, although he was on the baddie side of the equation a lot of the time," Rowan flashed a smile at the young man to show he was teasing, "so he didn't really know either. But it's basic psychology. Pack members need food, shelter, and to feel safe. With the exception of the elders and the people who thought Percy shit

134

golden cupcakes, no other pack member has had that. That's what you have to give them."

"Which means doing what exactly?" Shadow asked.

"I've got the list here." Rowan dug it out of his pocket.

/~/~/~/~/

The hall was in disrepair. It was just as well it was a dry evening, otherwise Shadow would be handing out umbrellas. From the rotten floorboards on the stage, to the ragged net curtains that were brown with dirt, it was clear no one had been in the community hall for years.

Standing in front of over a hundred people wasn't a new thing for Shadow. He'd trained men in the military, given the troops under his command a pep talk when necessary, but looking around at his audience now, he wasn't sure what to say. Men, women, children; most of them family groups although there were a group of teens standing across the wall at the back. The one thing they had in common was they were all looking at him expectantly. Wary, suspicious, and worn down. *What a fucking mess,* he thought grimly.

Shadow caught Rowan's grandmother's eye. She alone was smiling, along with two of her friends. On the other side of the hall stood four of the five elders. It seemed no one called Elder Clinton home after all. The rest was a sea of faces, some he recognized, others he didn't. It was clear not a lot of the pack recognized him. He held up his hands for quiet.

"Pack members, for those of you who don't know me, my name is Shadow, eldest son of Alpha Patrick. Many of you might remember me as Gray. Yesterday," *fuck, has it only been a day,* "Yesterday my father handed over the responsibility of the pack to me. I'm sure you've heard rumors of his long-term health issues. Regretfully, those are true. Your former alpha is currently in a rest home in advanced stages of canine dementia."

It was interesting that only a few of the older members showed any sign of remorse or sadness about his father's condition.

"You should also know, one of my first acts as your new alpha, was to kill my brother Percy and four of his goons who were caught engaging in abusive acts towards one of our own."

That elicited more of a response – the crowd nudging each other and whispering, while the elders looked wary. "You will find, that despite my military background, and the alpha training my father gave me before I left, that I do not condone violence of any kind except as quick and necessary punishment against those bullies who mistreat those weaker among us. I don't expect you to trust this yet, but hopefully over time you will see the truth of my words."

Shadow glanced over to Rowan who was standing with Marco, Craven, Dominic and Talon. Rowan gave a small nod, Marco gave him a thumbs up, but that support was enough for

Shadow to continue. He turned back to the pack.

"It breaks my heart to come home and see the pack in such disrepair. However, there is no point in dwelling on what has happened, or who was responsible. My father is beyond making restitution to anyone, and my brother is dead. It is my hope that we can all work together to bring this pack, and our territory back to its former glory."

Looking down at the piece of paper, lovingly etched in his mate's handwriting, Shadow said strongly, "It is with this end in mind, the following changes will be made, effective immediately."

"Excuse me, Alpha *Gray*, is it?" Elder Simon raised his hand. "The elders weren't consulted about any changes you were going to make. Indeed, we weren't even formally notified the pack had changed hands. It was a huge shock to be told we had to attend this evening without being spoken to beforehand."

Shadow could feel his wolf lurking behind his eyes. "The name is Shadow," he bit out. "Gray was a hopeless kid who believed the lies he was told by his father about how only the strong survive. I was named by my army friends, who saw me for who I was and what I could do. I am not the child you watched being raised here anymore. Furthermore, you elders were not consulted because a brief study of the pack finances this afternoon shows you four are part of the problem. You should know, I've commissioned a full audit of all the monies paid to you for pack services. I will be demanding to see evidence of how that money was spent bettering the lives of the pack, as it was intended to do. Should any of you be found to have used a single cent of that money for personal gain or benefit, you will face the pack and answer for your crimes."

Yeah, I thought that would shut you up, Shadow thought as Simon tried to blend in with the walls. He faced the rest of the pack. "Effective immediately, the pack tithe rate is reduced to five percent of household income, *per household,* not per individual as it was before. For those of you struggling to pay that amount, there will be hardship forms available in the new community office being opened in two days' time."

Shadow had wanted to put off the paying of tithe's completely, seeing as the system had been abused so badly, but Rowan convinced him that pack members took pride in contributing what they could afford.

"Secondly," he continued, "There will be no rents payable on the houses currently owned by my family being used exclusively for pack members. This will also come into effect immediately. It has come to my attention that some of you have had family homes sold out from under you, under Percy's orders and where possible I will be buying them back for you. Any of you directly impacted by this, there will be forms for that at the community office too. You and your families have a right to be secure in your homes and I will do my best to honor that."

That did generate more excitement and Shadow could see some of the men and women with children doing the math in their heads. With a lot smaller tithe, and no rents to pay, financially their lives were going to be a lot easier. Shadow only hoped that some of the pack would use the extra money to make improvements on their home. It seemed some of the pack members were feeling the same way.

"Alpha." A woman stepped forward, a small child clinging to her hip. "Meaning no disrespect, but I have to ask. Does this mean I can get my mate to fix our roof now? Only, none of us dared fix anything before, because if we did someone would come along and charge us a tax on the repairs."

Shadow could only guess who was demanding the tax and he cursed his brother under his breath. "Can I ask who you are? I do recognize some of you, but it's going to take a while for me to put names to all of your faces."

"Molly Tyne, Alpha." Molly respectfully tilted her head to one side. "My mate is Robby Tyne, and we have three children. Devin here is our youngest."

"You have a lovely family," Shadow said honestly. Molly looked tired, and far too thin for her age and the fact she'd had children, but the children were all clean and clearly cared for. Her mate hovered behind her protectively but didn't do more than tilt his neck in Shadow's direction.

"You can tell your Robby to order the supplies for the roof tomorrow, and for him to book them up to a new pack account that will be opened first thing in the morning. That goes for all of you," Shadow added, addressing the crowd. "If you have house repairs that need doing, and you're happy to do the work yourselves, then all of the materials will be supplied by us. If you need a qualified tradesperson, and you can't work out a barter between yourself and other pack members, then there will be request

142

forms you can submit at the community office to get the work done."

"Someone is going to be buried under a mountain of paperwork," Molly said with a smile, and then she blushed. "Sorry, Alpha."

"No apologies needed," Shadow smiled. "You are right. Unfortunately, I can't wind back time, or wave a magic wand and make all of our problems disappear in five minutes. There is a lot of work the inner circle and I need to do. Our first priority will be to clear out Rogue Alley and claim back our land there. I will, over the next week or so, be visiting you all at your homes, so you will all get your chance to talk to me personally about changes you want to see in this pack. For now, I have already allocated the funds the school had been asking for, ensured the food bank will be stocked by tomorrow morning at the latest, and workers will be coming in to help fix up this hall early next week."

It was actually Dominic who'd done all that, while Shadow had been with his mate, but Shadow felt it was important the pack know their Alpha and inner circle were working for the betterment of the pack.

The mood in the hall was a lot lighter now. Shadow could feel it, and he mentally thanked his mate for his list. Rowan was right. Most of the pack members did just want a chance to better themselves and their homes. He was just about to introduce his mate and the members of his inner circle, when someone else pushed forward. The man looked to be in his mid-twenties, which wasn't much of an age indicator, given he smelled strongly of wolf, among other things. But the surly expression on the man's face, caused Shadow's wolf to bristle.

"How you gonna do all this, aye?" The man snarled, slouching with his hands deep in his pockets. "I see only two of your military buddies, sharing the stage with a traitor and a no-good omega. You might have thought your fucking brother ran this pack, but he was just a petty nuisance. There're forces lurking around the fringes of this pack, strong forces that don't give a shit about fixing roofs or feeding mealy mouthed kids who don't give nothing back. You don't know nothing about them, or what they'll do and if that's the best you can do for an inner circle, you are going to end up fertilizing the pine trees within a week."

"That sounds a hell of a lot like a threat to me." Shadow flexed his fists, showing his claws, determined to eviscerate the man if he said one thing further.

Rowan's yell stopped him. "Shadow, don't, please. Harry doesn't mean to sound like that." Shadow heard him limping over, although he refused to take his eyes off the threat. Rowan's hand was a comforting weight on his arm. "Harry's not threatening you. He's telling it like it is, as he sees it, like a lot of people from Rogue Alley see it. His son, his only son Bart died because of some bad drugs only six months ago. Harry had already lost his wife when Bart was born. That boy was the only thing in his life, and drugs took him. Drugs that were pushed onto pack members by Percy and a handful of others in this pack."

"Human drugs don't work on shifters." Shadow willed his claws away. Harry's surliness had dropped the moment Rowan mentioned his son's name and now Shadow could see the man's grief for what it was.

"They do if they're cut with wolfsbane," Harry said sadly. "My boy, my poor boy. He just wanted to fit in. I begged Percy. I gave him absolutely everything I had, including the house if he'd just leave my boy alone. But your brother laughed at me. Took everything I offered and then told me it was Bart's choice. Next thing I know Bart is Percy's new best friend. Two months later he was dead."

"I will ensure you get restitution," Shadow said quietly, although he knew nothing would ever make up for losing a son. "I've already said, I can't change things overnight, but the one thing I will not allow in this pack is drugs of any kind. I need you to help me, Harry. Can you do that? Can you come to Rogue Alley with me and help me weed out these forces you talk about?"

"I'd take them out myself if I could. I tried once." Harry pulled his left hand out of his pocket. Only there wasn't a hand, just a stump at wrist level where his hand should be. "There's just some folks that don't like being told no more."

Shadow closed his eyes, but only briefly. The crowd was hushed, and he knew what he said next was going to be pivotal for getting the decent members of his pack on his side.

"I meant what I said, Harry, and I'm telling all of you others as well. From now on, this pack and my territory is a drug free zone. If you don't like it; you'd better get off my land. If I find one illicit drug anywhere, see one person under the influence, spot one individual selling that shit on my streets, and in our homes, then they will be dead. There will be no second chances for that. I can forgive a lot of things, but the abuse of the weak, and drugs are two things that will not be tolerated. At all."

"Yeah, well, I can see you mean well," Harry said, showing his neck before straightening again. "I still don't see how you're going to accomplish all this, especially with that traitor and the omega..."

"Stop right there, Harry. The rest of you need to hear this, too." Shadow slung his arm around Rowan's shoulders as he looked around his pack mates, then indicated to Talon who was standing close behind his mate. "Talon is no traitor. He's admitted his wrong doings and has agreed to work with me to make things right again. You should also know, the omega Rowan, is the only reason I came back to this territory. I knew he was my mate before I left, and I spent ten years away, allowing him time to grow up into the amazing shifter you see in front of you today. Yesterday, Rowan accepted my claim on him, and agreed that we are fated for each other. Omega, he might be, but he is also the Alpha Mate of this pack. He will be treated with the respect that position deserves."

Harry looked non-plussed for a moment, and then he let out a chuckle, a chuckle that developed into a full belly laugh. "Oh, my goodness," he said when he could finally talk. "Those forces that lurk in the shadows had better watch the fuck out. All shifters know how much stronger an alpha can be when he's true mated to his omega. That is the best news I've heard in ages. This pack finally has a chance. Kneel everyone. Kneel and show your respect for our new alpha pair."

Harry was the first one on his knees, his head tilted to show off his grubby neck. One by one the rest of the pack followed with the exception of the elders, who quietly slipped out of the hall. *I'll deal with them tomorrow,* Shadow promised himself as he bid his new pack to get back on their feet again.

Chapter Eleven

"It's been four days," Rowan grumbled as he jabbed the escape key on his keyboard with more force than necessary. "If I wanted to spend my time alone, I could've stayed single."

"You are the one who insists on working at your own apartment," Talon pointed out calmly. "And what am I? A hunk of wood?"

"I'm grateful you're here," Rowan said, staring at his screen and seeing nothing at all. "You playing my newest game for me has been really helpful in my ironing out a few bugs it had. It's just..."

"You miss your alpha," Talon shrugged as he continued playing his game. "I don't know why you just don't tell him to stay home once in a while. The pack's been a mess for years. He's not going to fix everything overnight."

"Huh, try telling him that." Rowan tried not to let his bitterness swamp him, but for all Shadow's agreement that Rowan was alpha mate, and he should have a part in anything the alpha did, the damn man still managed to be out of bed and be gone before Rowan woke up in the morning. "I'm worried," he said, tapping his finger nails on the desk. "I've had this horrible feeling in my gut since Shadow said he was going after those drug dealers – you know, the ones who've been squatting in those empty houses on Rogue Alley?"

"Damn it," Talon cursed as the game played that annoying wah-wah noise it made when a character died. "I almost made it to level twelve."

"You were supposed to stock up on power levels, food, and weapons before you left level ten. Talon, I'm worried about Shadow!"

Pushing back from the corner of the desk he'd made his own, Talon disappeared into Rowan's kitchenette and started making a pot of coffee. Rowan's eyes narrowed and he swiveled in his chair, so he was facing the kitchen. "You know something, don't you? That's why you're not answering me. Something's going down today, and you've been told not to say anything about it to me. I'm right, aren't I?"

"Up until now, I don't recall you asking me a question. You're all, 'I'm worried about Shadow, I've got these squishy feelings in my tummy and it's got nothing to do with the fact I haven't eaten anything except half a dozen power bars since breakfast'. Which aren't good for you, by the way. The packaging on those bars might say they are designed to bring you maximum energy, but they're just full of sugar. Read the ingredients label on the back."

Rowan growled. Nothing as impressive as he'd heard Shadow do, but neither he nor his wolf was happy with the way Talon was acting. He decided to go for the direct approach. "Talon, is anything Shadow is planning to do today dangerous?"

"Define dangerous," Talon said, but Rowan noticed he was making a real meal out of filling the coffee machine.

"Fine." Rowan stood up and plucked his jacket off the back of the couch. "Leave the coffee, I'm going out." He put on his jacket and headed for the door.

"Cool," Talon said, abandoning the machine and grabbing his own bulky jacket. "Where are we going, because I could murder some lunch."

"I'm sure my grandmother will make something for you," Rowan said brightly, checking to make sure he had his keys before opening the door. "She's always got stuff on hand to make me a sandwich when I've wanted one. Come on."

"Hang on." Talon's grip on his arm was light. "We're going to visit your grandmother? But, it's only Thursday. You visit your grandmother on Fridays when you take her baking stuff. I should know. I watched you do it often enough."

"And that's not creepy at all," Rowan teased as he shrugged off Talon's hand and walked out the door. "I don't need to take her anything for baking anymore. Craven set up an account for her, and they are making regular grocery deliveries every week in payment for her baking for the kids all these years. Which means, I can go and visit her anytime I like. It'll be fun. Close the door on your way out."

"Rowan," Talon fumbled with the door, and then hurried after him. "Your gran lives on Rogue Alley."

"I know." Rowan walked outside and unlocked his car. Holding the driver door open, he waited for Talon to get to the passenger side. "But you and Shadow have taken great pains to tell me how much safer it is there now. It's broad daylight. We're only going to my grandmother's house. I'm not inviting you to an orgy."

"I'd rather take the orgy," Talon muttered. "Look, why don't we go and have lunch in town, and visit your grandmother later. She's probably got friends visiting. She might not even be home. That's it. Why don't you call her first, and make sure she's there?"

"You want me to call my own grandmother and make an

appointment to see her?" Rowan laughed as he got into the car and put the keys into the ignition. "Get in Talon. My grandmother's always happy to see me no matter what time or day I visit her."

Talon got in the car, but instead of putting his seat belt on, he reached over and grabbed the car keys, wrenching them from the ignition and shoving his hands, with the keys under his armpits. Given he had four inches and about fifty pounds on Rowan, Rowan didn't see much chance of him getting them back.

"You can't go to your gran's house just yet," Talon said firmly, staring out of the front windscreen. "If you want lunch, and lord knows I do, I'll give you back the keys and we'll go to the food truck at the bottom of Princess Street. All right? Trust me on this."

Rowan eyed his friend cautiously. Everything in Talon's behavior indicated he knew something was going on and he wasn't going to say anything. "I want lunch." He held out his hand for the keys.

"You want lunch at the food truck on Princess Street." Talon dangled the keys just out of reach.

"Fine, if you're going to be difficult. I want lunch at the food truck on Princess street," Rowan parroted, waving his hand under Talon's nose.

Talon frowned but dropped the keys into Rowan's hand. Rowan smirked, putting the keys into the ignition and starting the car. He reversed out of his parking spot, pointed the car down the road and hit the accelerator. *One... two... three...*

"Town is the other way," Talon said quickly. "Stop the car, Rowan."

"I know where town is," Rowan said, increasing the pressure on the accelerator pedal slightly. "But I'm not going to town. I'm going to my grandmother's house." He flashed a saucy smile in Talon's direction. "We'll go to the food truck at the bottom of Princess Street for lunch, *tomorrow*."

"Damn it all to fucking hell." Reaching over, Talon yanked hard on the handbrake that sat between them. The car lurched to a sudden stop. Rowan flopped back in his seat, his heart pounding after almost cracking his head on the steering wheel.

"What on earth do you think you're doing? You could've caused an accident." Rowan quickly checked the rear vision mirror. Fortunately, he lived on a quiet street and most of his neighbors were out during the day.

"You're not leaving me a lot of options," Talon said fiercely. "I had one job today. Just one. Keep the alpha mate from Rogue Alley, they said. Just for today, they said. That's all I had to do, and now you're going to make me lose the first home I've had in ages, and my job too because you're just being stubborn."

"You won't lose your job or your home," Rowan said, feeling a bit better now his heart was under control again. "For fuck's sake, Talon, you have to tell me what's going on. That bad feeling in my gut isn't going away. If anything, it's getting worse. My wolf's telling me there's something wrong with our mate and I demand, as your alpha mate, that you tell me what the hell is going on!"

"I promised I wouldn't say anything." Talon sounded miserable now, and Rowan felt bad for behaving like a two-year-old trying to get his own way. But the agitation his wolf was feeling was very real. He had to know what Shadow was doing.

"Talon, please. Who're they? Shadow, Craven and the others?"

Talon nodded.

"Okay, so there's something going down today, in Rogue Alley, and Shadow's leading whatever it is, and I assume he's told my grandmother to go out for the day, am I close?"

Talon nodded again.

"Right, so now we're getting somewhere." Rowan looked around. They were still stopped in the middle of their lane. "I'm going to move the car..."

Rowan stopped as the sound of a huge explosion rocked the sky. Looking up, he could see huge clouds of black smoke billowing through the air, coming from the direction of Rogue Alley. "Oh, my gods, Shadow!" Leaping from the car, Rowan started running down the road as fast as his legs could carry him. He'd barely made it ten feet and his bad leg crumpled under him. He knew the logical thing would be to get back into the car and drive to Rogue Alley. But all he could feel was Shadow's fear, his anger, and a shaft of pain. His wolf was howling, begging to be let free, but he wasn't on pack territory. The chances of being seen were too great.

"Rowan," he heard Talon yell for him, but he ignored it. All he could see was that cloud of smoke, and the hint of flames licking the edges of it. He stumbled along; his eyes wet with tears. *I've got to...*

"ROWAN! Look out!"

The sounds of scuffling behind him, made Rowan turn. He saw Talon fighting off two men dressed in black, wearing ski masks. He cried out, knowing he had to try and help his friend, but before he could even move, he felt a sharp twist in his ankle as his leg gave out completely. He hit the ground, barely registering the sidewalk beneath him and suddenly his head was covered in a dark cloth bag. Struggling fiercely, the pain in his ankle shooting up his leg, Rowan quickly found his hands tied behind his back. A dull thud sounded behind him and then pain bloomed along his skull. *Fuck, Talon, I'm so sorry. Shadow, where the fuck are you?* But then, as what often happens with a sharp pain in the head, Rowan knew no more.

Chapter Twelve

"Well, that didn't go to plan," Shadow said disgustedly as he brushed ash and soot off his new and ridiculously expensive suit. He looked around, surveying the huge clumps of metal and concrete strewn across the block. He tapped his ears, first one side and then the other, trying to alleviate the ringing he had in them. "Report," he ordered. "Is anyone hurt?"

"A few scrapes and bruises. Nothing that won't heal with a shift," Marco came over, combing what looked like splinters out of his bushy beard and hair. "Craven's in among the wreckage now in his wolf form, trying to sniff out why we missed the stink of gunpowder. We should have smelled that well before the door was even opened."

"Yeah, well these shits clearly know about us and what we are, which is all the more reason they need eliminating." Shadow quickly checked the rest of his team. Craven's dark shape was picking through the wreckage and Dominic was helping

Harry to his feet. The man appeared shaken, and he was going to have a wicked bruise on his head. "Harry, I thought you said this informant didn't know about us being shifters, or who we were."

"I also told you, I got the information about the asshole we were supposed to meet, secondhand from one of the younger guys in the pack. It was him that set up the appointment, not me. Damn fool idea, if you ask me." Harry scowled as he brushed concrete dust off his clothing. "If I hadn't have heard that click the moment dickhead Dominic here opened the door without so much as a sniff of what might be behind it..."

"I know, I know. Thank you for saving our lives." Shadow rubbed his hand across his face, his fingers coming away covered in dust. "The fact someone was trying to kill us is obvious. This was supposed to be a meet and greet, and then we were going to a 'buy' not a fucking execution. But who's behind this? A human or someone in the pack?"

"You've got something else you need to worry about," Dominic said grimly. "In case you've forgotten, you've got an alpha mate who's been grumbling to Talon that his newly claimed mate doesn't talk to him or let him know what's going on."

"He can't know about this," Shadow said quickly. He didn't want to think what Rowan would say if he knew Shadow and his friends had set up a meeting with drug dealers. It was why he'd purposefully blocked their bond and suppressed his wolf before the meeting was even scheduled to start. He needed to come across to the scumbag drug dealer as human as possible.

"And you don't think he'll find out?" Marco shook his head. "For fuck's sake, Shadow, there's a big assed hole where the road outside Rowan's gran's house used to be. He's not blind."

"Gas leak?" Shadow shrugged. "It was just fortunate the squatters are gone, and Rowan's grandmother is providing food for the builders over at the community hall today. Fuck. This is one hell of a mess."

"Yeah, well you've got an even bigger mess coming," Marco said, as the wail of sirens could be heard coming nearer. "Craven, get your damn clothes on, we've got company coming." The big wolf gave one last sniff and then loped off around the back of Rowan's grandmother's house.

"As for you," Marco said, slapping Shadow on the chest. "You need to think long and hard about the damage you're doing to your mating, by not keeping that sweet omega of yours fully informed. If these bastards are after you, and I'd bet next month's salary they are, then Rowan's in danger. The whole pack knows who he is, and that the two of you are true mates. If we've got issues with pack members..."

"Then they'll know what I'll do, or what I'd be prepared to give up, to keep Rowan safe." Shadow sighed. A large fire appliance rattled down the alley, closely followed by another truck, men pouring out of both as they swarmed the scene. Two police cars also arrived and suddenly the area was crowded. "I know. I'll talk to him - I'll talk to him tonight, or just as soon as we've gotten rid of this lot."

Straightening his jacket, Shadow kept his shoulders back, as he approached the most officious looking gentleman. "My name is Shadow Bronc. I own the land around here and was present for a meeting when the explosion happened. What can you guys tell me about the cause of this mess? Me and my business associates could've been killed." As Shadow's father always used to say – the best defense is a good offense every time.

Listening to the Fire Department Chief drone on about possible issues in the sewer pipes, Shadow opened his link with his mate, wanting to reassure himself Rowan was safely in his apartment where he should be. He frowned as his wolf came up with nothing. In fact, his wolf wanted out, frantically, annoyed Shadow hadn't paid heed to the warnings he'd been trying to give. *Which can only mean something's wrong with my omega. Fuck it all to hell.*

"Excuse me, Chief," Shadow said as soon as he could get a word in edgewise. "I'm sure your investigators know what they're doing. My apologies, but I have another urgent appointment. Can I introduce you to Dominic Stiles, my second in command? He has full authority to take your report and will co-operate fully with all aspects of your investigations."

Without waiting for the man to reply, Shadow waved Dominic over, then signaled Marco and Craven to his side as he strode from the scene. "I can't sense Rowan at all," he muttered as soon as they were out of earshot from everyone else. "We don't have a direct mind link, but I can always get a sense of where he is and what he's doing. I blocked our link earlier, and shut down my furry side, but now, I'm getting nothing from Rowan, and my wolf wants out in the worst way."

"Could be, your sweet mate has had enough of being treated like a fairy tale red riding hood who needs his hand held to go to the bathroom. He could have blocked your link when he realized you'd done it to him," Marco said grimly as he and Craven kept pace with him.

"He wouldn't do that, and even if he could, our wolves should still be able to sense each other. Mine is going frantic." Shadow broke into a run. The SUV they'd used to go to a meeting which had blown up in a spectacular fashion, was currently buried somewhere under the wreckage. Rowan's place was closer than the pack house from where they were. He picked up the pace, his friends keeping up with him easily.

Nothing could be heard but the sound of their boots pounding the uneven sidewalk, and harsh breathing. Shadow wasn't worried about his friends – they were all fit, as was shown by how easily they kept up. But his mind couldn't stop churning; worry about his mate interposed with how close they'd all come to dying that day.

Harry had been right. Shadow had been too full of his own importance, getting his mind straight for the role he was about to play of arrogant dealer with more money than brains. Marco and Craven had been scanning the street, looking for possible traps – just like any other scumbag would order his minions to do when they're on unfamiliar territory. It was Dominic who had knocked on the door, Harry by his side, Playing the role of middle man nicely. Feelings of anguish cut deeply through Shadow as he thought about what could have happened if Harry hadn't quickly shoved Dominic to the ground, covering his body with his own, the moment he heard that clicking sound. *Me and my men owe our lives to Harry. My mate's life too. Rowan would have surely died if the explosion had killed me.* If they had stepped inside the old apartment block...

Rowan's at his apartment, Shadow had to focus on something positive and Rowan was the only positive that mattered. *He'll be working on his computer, lost in his little world of coding. The moment he looks up at me, my cock will stand to attention. He'll say something sweet and cute like 'are you here to have lunch with me,' and I'll sweep him up, hold him close and then I'll sit him down and tell him...*

"That's his car," Craven yelled, pointing down the road.

Shadow looked up, so focused on putting one foot in front of the other, he hadn't noticed they were on Rowan's street. Rowan's car was parked at an odd angle, almost blocking one side of the road. Shadow could already see the car was empty, both front doors of it left wide open. Sprinting over, he could see the keys were still in the ignition.

"He could've seen the explosion," Marco said, pointing to the smoke that still lingered on the horizon. "If he was driving down here, when the explosion went off..."

"That doesn't explain where he is now, or why Talon's gone too," Shadow snapped. *I should've told him, I should've begged him to just stay in his apartment, just for today.*

"Talon had orders not to say anything, but the direction of Rowan's car suggests he was heading to his gran's anyway." Craven sniffed the air. He was standing around the passenger side of the car. "I'm picking up two strange scents with Talon's. No way of knowing if they're human or pack because one of the strangers uses far too much cologne."

"Spread out and see what else you can find," Shadow said grimly as he searched the ground for any possible clue. "Something made my mate leave his car..."

"Yeah, probably worried about you getting your ass blown up." Marco joined him, bending over sniffing the ground. Together they traced Rowan's scent from when he left the car, to about twenty feet away.

"Another scent. This one's wolf," Shadow snarled.

"It could have been another pack member, helping them." Craven joined them. "Smelling the ground's not going to tell us if they've been taken by force or not, and with this damn roading, there's no sign of a scuffle. Maybe they saw the explosion, had car trouble and someone gave them a lift."

"Excuse me," A woman's voice called out from about three houses down from where they were. "Excuse me, are you looking for the two men in that car over there?"

"Why yes, ma'am, we are." Marco must have known how close Shadow was to losing his shit as he moved in the woman's direction, taking the lead on talking to a potential witness to whatever happened to his mate. "The young man who was driving the car is a good friend of ours. We had plans to meet up for lunch, but he never arrived."

"I knew something had happened, and I did call the police," the woman, a lady in her mid-thirties who was still wearing a night robe, had red around her nose and eyes, indicating she probably had a cold. "I'm not usually home through the day," she said to Marco, although Shadow could hear her clearly.

"I've been sick and was asleep. But there was that huge explosion. It was so loud it rocked the bed. I got up, like you do, and I was peering out the window when I saw your friend's car was parked like it is in the middle of the road. I thought, 'well, that's not right' and I was just going out to see if I can help, when I heard this voice yelling really loudly."

"That was very sweet of you to want to help," Marco said gently. "Could you hear who was yelling and what they were saying?"

Now the woman's cheeks were as red as the puffiness around her nose and eyes. "There wasn't much to hear. I just heard one young man, he was on the passenger side of the car yelling out to Rowan is it, at least that's what it sounded like, and telling him to watch out."

She clutched at the front of her robe. "I couldn't go out then, I was too scared. That one guy by the car who was yelling for his friend was fighting really hard against two other guys. I thought he was winning, but he was trapped by the car door and then one of the attackers smashed the guy's head into the door frame. He just collapsed in a heap on the ground and the two men started to drag him away. I was talking to the police by this time. I mean, you don't expect to see things like that in this street."

"I agree, ma'am, that must have been really frightening for you," Marco soothed.

What about Rowan? Because it was clear to Shadow from what he'd heard, that it was Talon fighting off the two men and he must have been unconscious for anyone to be dragging him away.

"Did you see what happened to the other young man?" Marco continued calmly. "He has a bad leg and limps sometimes, maybe you noticed?"

"Oh, that poor dear. I see him sometimes when he's collecting his mail and I'm heading to work. He has such a lovely smile." The woman shook her head. "He was crying and sobbing so loud I could hear it, staring at the smoke above the buildings, shouting something that sounded like Shadow. His leg gave out on him. It was like he was stumbling towards the explosion, which makes no sense at all. But then he fell, and his friend yelled at him to look out, but it was too late by then. There was a third stranger in a mask looming over him. They put a black sack over his head."

Shadow could feel his wolf rising, not taking no for an answer. His mate, his sweet mate thought something had happened to him and... And...

"Ma'am, this is very important," Marco said urgently. "Did they get in a car, or a van, or some kind of transport? They must have done, surely, if you saw the two men being dragged away."

"A black van." The woman sniffed and nodded, dabbing at her nose with a tissue clutched in her hand. "I got the number plate. I gave it to the police, but the lady on the phone said that all available patrol cars were being rerouted to the explosion site, and they didn't have any patrol cars in the area. I told them to hurry. I told her men were being kidnapped off the street in broad daylight, but all she could say was that someone would get back to me."

Craven and Shadow shared a knowing glance. It was clear the whole thing had been planned and whoever took Rowan knew Shadow and his friends would be at the site of the explosion.

The helpful neighbor was crying now. "I mean, I tried, didn't I? I gave them the plate number, I told them the crime was happening right then and there, but no one came to help. How does that happen? Here, of all places. This is a nice street, although maybe this is the cheaper side of town, but surely..."

"Ma'am, you've been immensely helpful," Marco said, gently taking her arm and leading her back to her house. "If you could just give me the plate number you gave to the police, me and my friends will go down to the precinct and see what's being done about those two young men. You don't have to worry about it anymore. You've done so much already."

"But I don't think I did..." Her voice trailed off as Marco got her into her house.

"A plate number's better than nothing," Craven said grimly.

"I will kill them," Shadow promised. "I don't care who or what or why, I'm going to kill them all. Endangering my pack by blowing up part of my territory was one thing, but if just one lock of hair on my sweet mate's head doesn't curl the way it should, I am going to tear apart those who took him, into such small pieces, there won't be enough for dental records to identify them."

"This could be an inside job," Craven warned as Shadow watched Marco stride out of the neighbor's house and head their way. "The explosion was one thing to try and kill us, but timing that with a hit on your mate is too much of a coincidence to ignore."

"If it's someone in my pack responsible for this, you can bet I'll know who they are by nightfall." Shadow curled his lip. "It's time to go hunting boys. I want every single pack member identified and located before night fall. I refuse to spend the night without my mate in my arms."

Chapter Thirteen

Rowan woke with a thumping headache and he winced as he tried to open his eyes. His vision was blurry, and it took quite a few blinks before he could see clearly again. Not that there was anything to see. It was pitch black all around him. His hands were still tied behind his back, but he'd been laying on something solid. Concrete, he guessed, coming from the chill underneath him.

He tried to push himself upright, into a sitting position, but with his hands behind him and his bad leg, he found it impossible. Wiggling his whole body backwards, his back encountered something wet and solid. *Eww, damp walls,* he thought as he used the wall to move his body, so he was at least sitting on his butt – on damp concrete - but it was better than laying like a sacrificial offering. Rowan shivered and it wasn't just from the cold.

As his brain slowly cleared from the fog he experienced when he woke up, Rowan's memories of being taken flooded his brain. He strained his ears, but the only sound he heard was his own heart, and subdued breathing. *What did they do with Talon?* Rowan hoped his friend was all right. His wolf could sense Shadow was alive despite the explosion which was one relief. If the man had died, as Rowan feared, his wolf would be inconsolable. *But he's busy as usual,* his brain supplied and that really wasn't helpful to Rowan's current state of mind.

Looks like it's just me and you, he sent to his wolf, who was strangely subdued. If anything, his wolf half seemed to be waiting, but for what was anyone's guess. Rowan huffed and wiggled his toes in his boots. At least he was still clothed, which he was going to take as a tick in the positive column. But the sharp pain that ran up his leg reminded him he'd twisted his ankle and his bad leg was throbbing badly thanks to the chill. *That means any form of running is out of the question.*

Rowan sighed and leaned back against the wall behind him. A cold seeping sensation came through his jacket almost immediately, and he bum-shuffled forward about a foot before he stopped. His hands being tied was the real issue. *Maybe I could bring them around to my front and get rid of the ties with my teeth.*

Rowan was sure he'd read of someone doing that once, but unfortunately, reality was a lot harder than fiction. *I'm going to have to lean on that bloody wall,* he thought, dreading the idea of his clothes getting any damper than they were. His goosebumps had goosebumps, and Rowan wished he could shift. But with his hands behind him, he'd just dislocate his shoulders if he tried, and besides, without knowing who'd taken him, it'd be a huge risk.

Sniff, smell, damn it. What can I smell? Not a lot, which wasn't helping his situation either. There was no scent of anyone in the hole he was in. Just damp, mold, and a slight chlorine smell from the water, Rowan guessed, or maybe the concrete itself. *Basement? Cold cellar?* Aside from the concrete, there were no other clues. Even after his eyes adjusted to the dark, all he could see was more concrete, shaped in a curve.

There's no door. No window. Fuck! Rowan's heart rate increased, and he started to pant. His mind went into overdrive, imagining himself buried somewhere in a concrete tomb where no one would ever find him. *Look up. Look up,* his logical mind screamed at him. Still hyperventilating, Rowan looked up. The ceiling curved up towards the middle. Small chinks of light shone around a dark circular shape at the summit of the wall curves.

I'm in a tank.

It's not covered in dirt.

There's no way in hell I can get out.

The tank was wide – easily more than two of Rowan's arm widths. From what he felt from leaning on the wall, Rowan knew the surface of the concrete was uneven, but as he was a wolf shifter and not a goat, he had no way of climbing even if his leg was in perfect shape.

Rowan's panic was there, right under the surface of his skin, threatening to erupt in a meltdown of epic proportions. His mind was running the statistics – days a body could live without food. How bad would his thirst have to be before he licked the walls. *Where would I pee,* because the thought of dying among his own muck wasn't helping Rowan's peace of mind at all.

I must get my breathing and heart rate back to normal. I'm going to get my hands free. It was the only thing remotely in his control. What he was going to do afterward was anyone's guess. Rowan's mind flitted to Shadow – a mate he barely knew and who'd become so distant over the past few days, it was like living with a stranger, which apart from the sex and Rowan's distant memories of an alpha's son, he was. *At least he's okay. It's such a damn shame he's too busy to notice I'm missing.*

/~/~/~/~/

"I will fucking kill you." Shadow threw the young man against the wall and then stalked after him. The asshole was easy to find. The cologne he wore could be scented by Craven even after Rowan's attacker had showered. It was a pack member, just as Shadow feared, but young, barely eighteen. His two co-conspirators were huddled in a corner crying.

Picking the man up again, Shadow held him high above his head wanting nothing more than to wring the man's scrawny neck. "I'm going to kill you and when I'm done, I'm going to tear every inch of flesh off your bones. I'm going to take those bones and grind them into a paste, and then I'm going to shovel that paste down your parents' necks before I banish them forever. Do you hear me?"

"We were ordered to do it." The young man's voice cracked, and he'd peed his pants. "I didn't want to. None of us did. But Dad always told me to obey the elders."

Fucking knew I should've dealt with them when I had the chance. Shadow mentally cursed. "Where. Is. My. Mate?"

"I don't know. Honest I don't." Tears and snot ran down the young man's face. "We... I... We were ordered to take them out to Elder Simon's house. He lives on the edge of pack territory. That's all we did. Just dropped them off. Honest. They were still alive when we left them there."

The "for now" was implied. Shadow shook the man's body hard, before launching him through the air again, sending him flying against the wall his friends were huddled against. "Lock 'em up," he snarled at Harry, well aware his fangs were showing. "If they so much as hint at running away, tear their throats out and leave their bodies for the rest of this pack to find. I will teach everyone what happens when they come between me and my mate."

Shadow turned, the urge to kill so strong in man and wolf, he had to get out of the house. He knew Rowan was alive, but that was all he knew. And it wasn't enough. Long shadows cast by the setting sun showed it would be nightfall soon. In his mind's eye, Shadow could see him. His poor mate huddled somewhere, most likely in the cold and dark. Hurt. Probably hungry. He strode over to his SUV, confident his three friends would follow him.

Chapter Fourteen

Rowan shivered, trying to keep his legs crossed as the pressure on his bladder increased. He rubbed his hands up and down his arms, the twin bands of blood around his wrists showing tearing a plastic tie with his teeth wasn't as easy as it looked on television. It'd been a real struggle, getting his hands in front of him, but while his wrists and shoulder's ached, he'd managed it. He had no idea how much time had passed. The shadows cast by the chinks of light in the ceiling had moved but weren't as strong as they were before. He never wore a watch and he'd left his phone at home. It wasn't as though Shadow ever called him. Rowan didn't think his mate even had his number.

I should've dated him before I let him claim me. Rowan's hollow laugh bounced off the concrete. It's not as though he'd ever dated anyone. Cassie used to date, a lot. Rowan remembered how she'd come running into his dorm room one time, holding up her phone like a trophy. "He gave me his number," she'd shrieked, bouncing on Rowan's bed. Like it was a big deal, just exchanging contact details and yet, Rowan would've given anything to have felt that one fissure of excitement, the promise of a new love, just once before he died.

Shadow is a good alpha. Rowan examined that statement, making a mental list of pros and cons. The problem, Rowan admitted to himself, was he didn't have many decent examples to compare Shadow to, in either the alpha or the mate sense. Shadow was better than his father in being alpha. And he was twenty thousand times better than his brother Percy. But then Percy wasn't alpha born. Rowan wondered if that's why Percy used to be such a shit. It couldn't be easy trying to live up to a perfect older *alpha* brother.

"This place is really getting to me if I'm thinking of Percy in a compassionate light." Rowan pushed himself to his feet, biting his bottom lip as his ankle throbbed. "I have to move, I have to move," he mumbled, hopped around, waving his arms up and down trying to generate some heat. "La, la, la, la, la, la," he yelled, wincing as the noise sounded so much louder as it echoed in the enclosed chamber.

"Oh, fuck it." Rowan levered himself back to the floor again, sticking out his bad leg and rubbing it, trying to soothe the aches away. He thought back to when Percy had held him for a week. He wasn't fed then, and only given a cup of water to drink a day. Percy wasn't trying to kill him, just torture him and then probably kill him, but Rowan's grandmother put the word out he was missing, and Percy let him go. It wasn't as though Rowan was going to tell anyone what he'd done.

Would it have been better if I had died then? Rowan quickly shut down his morbid thoughts. If he was going to die, it would take weeks and surely his grandmother would be missing him by then. *Not Shadow?* Rowan sighed in the gloom. Shadow would realize something had happened to him when he finally hit the bed later that night and he wasn't in it. But then, being the pragmatic and logical man that he was, Shadow would likely think he was simply working at his apartment.

"Silly bastard would probably think he was being considerate in not trying to get in touch with me, not wanting to disturb my work. Damn it." Rowan tried to think of something else. He was worried about Talon. He wondered what his grandmother was doing, but every thought he had meandered back to his hugely muscled, definitely lacking in romance, mate.

Oh, those muscles. Closing his eyes, Rowan allowed himself to dream of his sexy mate. At least thinking about him was keeping parts of his body warm although he still needed to pee. *What I could've done to you, if you'd only given me the chance,* he thought sadly.

/~/~/~/~/

Shadow didn't knock at the door. Hell, he'd barely waited for the SUV to stop before he was out, bounding up Elder Simon's porch, and smashing through his door like a tornado. "Where is he?" he snarled, shocking the Elder, his wife and three children who appeared to have just sat down to dinner. The smell of hot roast beef wiped out the sniff of Rowan's scent that he'd caught as he'd burst through the door. "Where's Rowan?"

"Alpha?" Simon touched his lips delicately with his napkin before setting it down on the table and getting to his feet. "I must admit this is a huge surprise. Won't you join us for dinner? My mate makes the most excellent rare roast."

"I wouldn't eat with you if you were the last piece of shit wolf on earth." Shadow curled his lip as he deliberately stripped off his shirt and tossed it at Marco who was standing to the left and just behind him. "Ma'am, I suggest unless you have knowledge of where my mate is, that you and your children barricade yourselves in your bedroom. Things are about to get ugly."

Simon's mate, to her credit, didn't say a word, simply getting up from the table and shepherding her children out of the room. Simon's gaze got more wary as he watched them go. "Alpha, I must protest," he started to say as soon as they were gone.

"I don't want to hear anything out of your mouth except the whereabouts of my mate." Shadow dropped his hands to his belt and started unbuckling it, the clink loud in the silence of the room.

"Alpha, come on." Simon edged around the table. Like clockwork, Marco, Dominic and Craven moved, blocking all the room's exits. "Look, you don't know what you're dealing with here..."

"I don't want to know. I want my mate." His belt unbuckled; Shadow then kicked off his boots. They flew up and then landed on the polished wood floors with a heavy thud.

"Alpha, Gray, Shadow, please. You've got to let me explain," Simon wailed, cringing backwards. "There's stuff going on here that have been years in the making. Deals with humans. Drug trafficking. Nothing to do with me. I'm just trying to maintain the status quo so no one gets hurt."

"I won't ask you again. Where's my mate?" Shadow warned. "You have just ten seconds to tell me what you did with my mate after your little foot soldiers dropped him and Talon off here, or I will rip your throat out. Ten... Nine... Eight..."

"They're out the back!" Simon cowered, raising his arms up to protect his head. "In the junkyard at the end of the back yard. You don't understand, if I don't give them something, they'll kill me. They said you had to be stopped."

Shadow didn't have a clue who 'they' were. He just needed his mate. Until Rowan was safe in his arms, he wasn't going to be able to think of anything or anyone else. "You can tell your friends to forget about stopping me. I'm just getting started," he snarled as he stalked barefoot out the door.

Running around the back of the house, Shadow spotted the junk yard fifty yards away, piled high with debris. Rowan's scent was faint, as though he'd been carried. Talon's scent was more pronounced and there were scuff marks in patches on the grass as if he was still fighting his captors. A rusted chain link fence divided the back lawn from the junk yard, and it was there the scents split up. "Dominic, Marco, find Talon." Shadow pointed to where Talon's scent was headed. "Craven, you're with me."

Moving around the piles of junk quickly wasn't easy. Old car bodies were stacked up in haphazard fashion, and there were iron bars, steel poles and engine parts scattered in piles across the uneven ground. The scent of gas, oil and cleaners battled with the faint traces of Rowan's smell, but Shadow persisted, sniffing in car bodies, leaning over until his nose almost hit the ground in some places, trying to get more of his mate's scent.

"Wait," Craven's hand landed on his arm. "Can you hear that? It's coming from over there." He pointed to the back of the yard where six huge concrete water tanks stood against the fence line.

Straining his ears, Shadow smiled for the first time that day.

"When you look at me, I can touch the sky, I know that I'm alive."

The voice was faint, off key and wobbling a bit on the higher notes, but Shadow would know that voice anywhere. "I don't want to hear anyone criticizing my mate's singing voice," he said with a smirk as he leaped over an old engine and sprinted towards the tanks.

/~/~/~/~/

"I'm alive," Rowan's voice wobbled, but he kept singing. "I can touch the sky. I'm alive, yeah, I'm alive. Yeah, I'm alive. I don't know for how long," he improvised to the same tune. "I'm as good as gone. I can't touch the sky, but I'm alive. I'm a... What the heck?"

Rowan could hear someone pounding on the concrete with what sounded like an iron bar. "Hey," he yelled as loud as he could, which wasn't easy with his throat dry from his spell at singing. "I'm in here." He slammed his open palms against the concrete wall. "I'm in here!"

Logic told him, the person outside wasn't necessarily the good guys, but Rowan was beyond caring. He could smell his own pee from when he was forced to go, his mood plummeting even as his bladder sighed in relief. It was why he was singing. Anything to take his mind off the pain in his leg, his grumbling guts and the horror he felt at having to sit in what was effectively his own toilet.

"Help, help," he yelled, hitting the concrete hard enough to make his palms bleed. "I can't get out. I can't get out!"

A loud grating noise sounded above him, and Rowan looked up, scared and relieved all at the same time. The cover to the opening of the concrete tank was dragged aside, and Rowan caught a glimpse of the pale pinks and bright yellows of the evening's sunset before a familiar face blocked his view.

"You've got no idea how glad I am to see you." Rowan said fervently, clutching his bloodied palms to his chest, his head tilted back as far as it would go.

"I know exactly how you're feeling, little red," Shadow's voice cracked slightly, and Rowan wondered if his mate was actually crying. But in the next sentence, Shadow was all business again. "Let me find a rope and we'll get you out of there."

Chapter Fifteen

Getting Rowan out wasn't as easy as simply dropping a rope down and him climbing up it like a monkey. The smell of Rowan's blood hit Shadow's nose as soon as he got the tank cover open. The pinched pale face, the way Rowan lurched and stumbled as he looked up, along with the blood Shadow could see on his palms and wrists all combined to create the picture of a man who was not going to be able to climb to freedom.

But when Shadow prepared to lower himself, determined to have Rowan in his arms as soon as possible, he was shocked by Rowan's yell. "Don't come down here."

"Babe, you can't climb the rope on your own. There's no weakness in being helped with that. You're injured. I need to help you." Rowan had no idea just how badly Shadow needed to help his mate. "I'm coming down." He nodded to Craven to hold the rope taut as he swung his legs into the hole.

"You can't come down here." Rowan was panicked, glancing to the side of the tank and wringing his hands. "It's not... I... It's not *nice* down here."

"I'm used to not nice." Shadow had a fair idea what was upsetting his mate. Blood wasn't the only smell his nose had picked up when the cover opened. But he wasn't going to discuss something so obviously distressing to his sensitive mate with the others hearing. "We'll have you out of there in a minute. Hang on."

Trusting his friend to have his back, and to ensure the rope didn't fray on the edges of the concrete, Shadow moved down the rope easily, his bare feet landing on something soft. "Rowan?" He looked down at Rowan's jacket that was under his feet, and then at his mate who was shivering in a thin t-shirt. "Oh, little red," he said with a groan, tugging his mate close and wrapping him in his arms. "If I had to wade through an ocean of piss to get to you, I would," he whispered against Rowan's ear.

"Please don't." Rowan's voice wavered and a splash of tears fell on Shadow's bare chest. "I thought I was going to die in a pool of my own pee if I was down here too long."

From the size of the tank, Shadow thought that was highly unlikely, but he was wise enough not to say so. He recognized the signs – his mate was cold, tired, hurt, and hungry. He was entitled to his breakdown. All Shadow could do was keep his mate close, letting his scent soothe Rowan's jagged nerves, while his body heat would help warm his mate's thin body.

Craven, to his credit, said nothing from his post at the top of the tank. Shouts Shadow could hear, indicated Talon had been found and he was spitting angry, and worried sick about Rowan. But it had to have been ten minutes, maybe more, before Rowan lifted his head and asked, "Are we going to stay in here all night?"

"I need you to climb on my back." Shadow used his hand to brush Rowan's curls back from his tear-stained face. "All you have to do is hang on, and I'll get us out of here."

"I'm so glad Talon's okay," Rowan said softly, sliding his hands around Shadow's waist as if he didn't want to lose contact. "It was my fault we were taken. He tried to stop me going to Rogue Alley."

"You got taken a couple of hundred meters from your house. Wanting to go to Rogue Alley had nothing to do with it." Shadow crouched down so Rowan could get a firm hold around his neck. He scowled as he saw the mess of Rowan's hands and wrists. "Hold on as best *you* can. I'll be as quick as *I* can."

Rowan didn't let out so much as a murmur as Shadow quickly climbed up the rope, although Shadow knew his mate was in pain. As he doubted Elder Simon had gently lowered Rowan into the tank in the first place, it was likely his mate was hurting more than he realized.

Grabbing Craven's hand as he reached the top of the tank, Shadow heaved himself out, reaching behind himself to pull Rowan back around to nestle against his chest. He ran his hands over every part of Rowan he could reach, noting every sharp inhale, or pained gasp. *Simon is going to pay for every bruise my mate has suffered,* he vowed.

"The alpha mate needs medical attention," Craven said quietly. "His boot looks like it's about to burst it's seams."

"I twisted my ankle. It's okay." Tears still clung to Rowan's long eye lashes, and Shadow vowed he'd do better as a mate. Hell, he was all for handcuffing his mate to his side and probably would've done, except Rowan's wrists were bruised and cut as well.

"We have a lot to talk about, you and I," he said gravely, brushing away a tear that fell down Rowan's cheek. "But you need food. You need rest..."

"I need to know you found Talon too, and then I need a shower," Rowan said with a burst of spirit, which must have cost him because the shadows were almost black under his eyes.

"A bath," Shadow could be just as firm. "You're not standing on that ankle until you've shifted. As for Talon, he's fine. Look for yourself." He pointed over the edge of the tank. Talon was in his wolf form sniffing around the edge of the concrete. Shadow had no doubt the canny wolf was memorizing scents and hoped Talon wouldn't be too upset that their attackers were still breathing.

Rowan peered over the edge and then snuggled back against Shadow's chest. "Please just take me home," he whispered. "I really can't take much more of today."

Shadow knew exactly how his sweet mate felt.

/~/~/~/~/

The Shadow who ran him a bath and gently tended to his wounds, was a totally different man to the one Rowan mated. His actions were slow and designed to soothe. The arousal so often present in his mate was in the air, but that was the only place it was noticeable. When Rowan opted for bed, rather than shifting as they waited for a meal, Shadow didn't push him to do otherwise. He simply nodded and reached for the biggest and fluffiest towel on the rack and dried him tenderly as if he was the most precious being on earth.

Even after they were in bed, and Shadow explained how the inner circle had worked to track down the drug dealers that seemed determined to make Rogue Alley their home, Shadow didn't flinch from his short comings, delivering his message in the same calm voice, even as he relayed Elder Simon's betrayal. Likewise, when Shadow voiced how he'd deliberately set Talon up to keep Rowan away from the action, his tone didn't change. He was telling it how it was, to him, as if Rowan would understand.

"Why?" Rowan asked when Shadow came to the end of his story. Inside, his mind was reeling over the duplicity of certain pack members and the worry that the lure of drugs and fast money had caused the rot in his pack to spread. But the pack wasn't in their bedroom. The damage done to his mating was the most important thing to Rowan in that moment. "Why did you keep all this from me? Why didn't you tell me what was going on? I would've stayed at home today, if I'd have known, then neither Talon nor I would've been taken. Didn't you trust me?"

"I trust you with my life," Shadow said, but he was staring at the wall beyond the foot of the bed, an action that didn't fill Rowan with much confidence. "Not telling you had nothing to do with how much I trust or care for you."

"I'm calling bullshit." Pushing Shadow's arm away from where it was draped over his chest, Rowan struggled to sit up. He wanted to see his mate's face, full on. "Your inner circle all knew about this investigation including the meeting you had planned for today. Hell, Harry knew and so did Talon. I bet even my grandmother knew..."

"She didn't know why it was better for her to be out of the house today,"

Shadow interrupted quickly. "I just told her I wanted her to help feed the workers at the community hall. That was it."

"Great, so my grandmother didn't know, but everyone else I've mentioned did. I'm the alpha mate. I thought that automatically made me part of the inner circle." Rowan reached out and turned Shadow's chin, so they were facing each other. It was the only way Shadow could feel the full brunt of his glare.

Like any ex-military man, Shadow didn't even flinch. "I know you're angry with me," Shadow started to say, but Rowan had had enough of his Zen mood.

"You have no idea how angry I am with you. I might look like a weak simpering omega who doesn't have two brain cells to rub together, but I have skills." Rowan wanted to punch Shadow's shoulder to make his point, but he didn't think his fist would make much of a mark and he didn't want to embarrass himself.

"Not only that, but I have every right, as the alpha mate, to be involved in every single decision that affects this pack, or my mate. You, running off to meet a known drug dealer, trying to pretend you're human – that's a joke and what's worse, it's the dumbest idea I've ever heard of. And I was right, wasn't I? It was a stupid idea because you damn near got yourself killed and what would have happened to me then? Drowning in my own piss would seem like a day at the park if you died. Don't you get it, you big lug? You could have DIED!"

Suddenly the enormity of the day's events hit Rowan hard. He started gasping, unable to catch his breath. He shuffled around on the bed, trying to open out his chest so he could breathe easier. But all that did was jolt his ankle, which sent pain screaming up his leg and into his thigh. And then suddenly that scream was everywhere. He opened his mouth, trying to take in more air, but his full-body scream came out instead.

Rowan couldn't stop. It was as though he was watching himself from the other side of the room. The sounds coming from him sounded like a pissed off banshee – his mouth was wide open, teeth exposed, his eyes were scrunched up and his nostrils flared seeking the air his chest couldn't take in. Rowan's face was so heated he thought his skin would split, and black spots filled his vision. He knew, on some cognitive level, he was going to pass out, but there was no way to put the brakes on what he was doing. Every slur against him since he shifted, all the pain Percy and his friends inflicted on him, the sheer terror at believing his precious mate had died that day all came out in one long, long, and incredibly loud scream.

Chapter Sixteen

Shadow's hand itched with the urge to slap his mate's face; it was standard practice against someone who was losing their shit as badly as Rowan was. But he couldn't bring himself to physically hurt his mate in any way. Rowan had a right to express his pain – a pain Shadow believed went far beyond the events of the day. But he was the root cause of it all. It was him that left his mate ten years before, hell bent on keeping his reputation intact, believing his pack mates would protect his mate. It was his arrogance that caused him to shut his mate out of what he was trying to do to weed out the trouble in his pack now he was home. Rowan's complete meltdown was his fault.

Which meant he was going to hug his mate through it. It didn't matter that his ear drums thought they would burst from the pitch coming from Rowan's mouth. Shadow's own heart, that felt as though it had cracked and was bleeding from the pain he caused, could be ignored for now. Gathering Rowan's shaking body close, he deliberately slowed his breathing, willing his heart to pump at a regular rate, projecting as much calm as he could through their frayed bond. *I am here for you. I am so sorry I let you down.* Shadow wished, with all that he was, that he and his mate enjoyed the mind link so common in alpha and omega pairings, and he had a fair idea why they didn't share one. His actions, since he claimed his wonderful mate, weren't those of a man open to their bonding, not to mention they weren't double claimed.

Rowan struggled in his arms. His poor face was almost purple. When the noise suddenly stopped as though someone had pressed a switch and Rowan's body went limp, Shadow instinctively raised his hand to the pulse in Rowan's neck. It was pulsing, harder than it should be, but Rowan was going to be okay. The skin under his fingers suddenly sprouted fur, and Shadow watched in amazement as Rowan's pure white wolf form came

213

through. *His poor wolf's protecting him.*

The wolf was alert, wary, his ears back and his shoulder's hunched as though expecting an attack. His bright eyes stared up at Shadow's face, and Shadow could see the caution in them. That, more than anything else, caused Shadow to crack. "I'm so sorry," he whispered, leaning over to press his forehead against that of his mate's. "I have not treated you like a good alpha should and for that I am truly sorry."

The wolf whined, but Shadow felt a wet tongue lick up his cheek.

"Would it help if I told you, I didn't know any other way of handling things? That it's in my nature to confide in my friends because I've always relied on them in the past? That I didn't tell you about my plans because I was seriously trying to protect you?"

Rowan's furry side grumbled. It wasn't a growl as such, but it was the rumblings of an animal who believed in being just as protective as Shadow had been.

"I know, I know. I was treating you like the precious human your other half is to me, but I should've known you wanted to protect me too."

Shadow got another lick for his confession. "This is all new to me, babe. I'm not trying to make excuses."

The chuff he got, reminded Shadow of when his mate had called him out on that same thing the morning after their first night together. "Okay, okay," he chuckled. "I get what you're saying, although at what point does an explanation become an excuse? Do you know? Because I sure as hell don't."

The wolf sniffed up his neck, and licked behind his ear, which was slobbery, but Shadow accepted the affectionate gesture for what it was. "It's the army life," he explained. "You have to depend on your friends, because if you don't then you'd be dead. Orders were strictly on a need to know. You reported to your superiors and kept your mouth shut with everyone else."

Shadow was having a bit of an epiphany. "You, my precious wolf, are a civilian. I mean, you're my mate," he added when Rowan nipped his ear lobe. Shadow ran his hand down Rowan's thick white fur. "You'll always be my mate, but when I saw the depth of the problem in this pack, I guess my army training kicked in. You should see my dad's old office. It's covered in maps, and pictures and..."

Rowan's whine made him realize what he'd said. "You're right." Shadow nodded. "You should have been in the office with me. I had no right to keep anything from you. And the only other *explanation* I can give you is that you've lived in this pack your whole life. I guess I didn't want you to see how far the corruption has gone among the people you care about."

The body under his hands shimmered, and he was touching skin again. "This is your home too,"

Rowan said fiercely, reaching up and framing Shadow's face with his hands. "This is not a military operation, it's a pack matter. You are the alpha of this pack. If there's shit going on here you don't like, you make those people accountable. Lock them up. Call in the guards and have them jailed. Banish them. Kill them if you have to, but act like an alpha instead of a general."

"I only made First Lieutenant," Shadow grinned. "Generals are the big wigs."

"I don't care what rank you were in the army. Here, you're the big wig. You don't report to anyone. You're it around here, and yes, we might live in a human world, but this territory is pure wolf and has been for decades. You own all the houses our pack lives in. It's your land that stretches around these houses allowing us to run. You are responsible for all the people, yes, but they have a responsibility to you too. It's about time they were reminded of that. The pack is meant to support their alpha."

"You're right, I know you're right." Shadow shook his head. "I just... it's just... I swear, I got back as soon as I could when I got the message from your gran telling me things had gone to shit for you. But I didn't plan for any of this. I never wanted to be alpha here. I wanted to take you away, with my friends and us start up a pack someplace else, quiet, peaceful, away from the fighting."

"The majority of this pack are good people." Rowan was deadly serious. "They didn't ask for the shit from your brother, and they didn't ask for the drug dealers who are sucking the life from this pack. Which reminds me. What makes you think the dealers are human?"

Shadow frowned. "It was obvious from the start. Paranormals don't deal in drugs, and besides the informant who set up the meeting told us that's what they are."

"That's the same informant who's currently sitting in the basement jail, along with his two friends after they kidnapped me and Talon today."

His mate did have a good point. "But everyone knows paranormals don't deal in drugs..."

Rowan held up his finger. "Everyone doesn't know that. Unless you've met every paranormal, you can't say that." He tapped the finger he was holding up. "One - the informant was working for Simon not humans." He tapped a second finger. "Two - a human wouldn't think to mask the scent of explosives at Rogue Alley. Three - humans wouldn't understand the mating bond between us. To humans at best I'd be nothing more than a boy toy and easily discarded. If they wanted leverage with you, they'd have stolen a pack female or a couple of kids. Four – Harry already told you the drugs that killed his son were laced with wolfsbane, which no typical drug dealers would think to use. And five," he tapped his little finger.

Fucking hell, my mate's right on every point. "Five?"

"Five – you said Simon showed real fear when he mentioned this mysterious person who wanted you out of the way. Simon wouldn't be afraid of a human, no matter how much of a thug the dealer might be. He might have a stick up his ass, and he's spent too long getting a tan to do this pack any good, but Simon's still a wolf shifter. An old one. Oh, and incidentally, I doubt Simon is the only elder involved in all of this. I'd say they all are, but I could be wrong about that."

"You've been right so far." Shadow leaned back against the headboard and slapped his own head. "Why didn't we see any of this?"

"Because you were thinking with your First Lieutenant brain, not the instincts of a wolf," Rowan said sharply. "This whole thing has been like a campaign in a war zone for you, but it's something much closer to home than that."

"What do you mean?" Shadow couldn't believe there was something else he might have missed.

"This is a pack takeover, pure and simple. Percy had been in charge roughly eight years. And in that time this pack has gone downhill badly. No one has any money; the pack members can barely keep themselves fed. The alpha, your father, was sick and barely hanging onto his sanity. Pack morale is at an all time low and that's without the drugs."

"I'm still not seeing a scenario for a pack takeover." Shadow loved the way Rowan's mind worked, but he had to be wrong on this, surely.

"The only reason your father was still alive when you got home, is because no matter what Percy did to this pack, he was only ever going to be a beta. If the council caught wind of his death, then Percy would have been out."

"The council would appoint another alpha to take my place if I couldn't be located," Shadow nodded, showing he was following Rowan so far.

"Which Percy definitely didn't want. But if another alpha, pride leader, or similar, made a deal with Percy to help run the pack with him, when your father did die..."

"Or was threatening Percy with a pack takeover, once my father was gone." Shadow's eyes widened as he stared at his mate – his very naked mate, who'd never looked more beautiful than he did when his smarts were showing.

Rowan shrugged. "I don't know the specifics. But there's another strong paranormal involved in all this somewhere, I'm sure of it. What I do know is, that no one knew the extent of your father's mental demise. Percy never let anyone see him, ever. Not even the elders."

"But the elders knew something was going wrong. They'd have to be blind to just keep accepting Percy's excuses for why he wasn't available all the time."

"True. But then why did you think they went on so many holidays?" Rowan rolled over and rubbed his stomach. "I need to see the tithe bank statements again, and a record of all the pack members. Food would be good too."

Shit. Shadow tore his eyes from Rowan's attractive junk and looked at his face instead. "You're tired. This can wait until tomorrow. Nothing's going to happen tonight."

"That's where you're wrong, mate of mine. Talon and I were rescued. Simon hasn't got anyone to hand over to whoever's behind this, unless he sacrifices his own wife and kids, and he won't do that. If he wasn't in jail, he'd be packing right now. If I were you, I'd find out why that food is taking so long and get it up here along with the papers I've asked for. And I'd also round up the other elders and put them in protective custody too."

Shadow double blinked. "Protective custody? That's what you're calling it?"

"If Simon was afraid, then you can bet the other elders are too. Taken out of their homes, separated so they can't collude..."

"You, my mate, are fucking brilliant." Shadow rolled over and pressed a hot kiss on his mate's head and then rolled the other way off the bed. "But I am going to insist, as your mate and alpha, that at some point in the very near future, you're going to allow me to explore that lovely body you're so happy to lay out in front of me."

Rowan's look could only be called sultry and Shadow felt the heat from it run throughout his whole body. "Given your alpha tendencies I'm thinking the next time we're intimate, you're going to agree to being tied to this bed, and to me doing the exploring. Now find me some pants."

"Yes, sir." Shadow grinned as he reached for the nearest dresser. Strangely enough, the idea of being tied up, perked his cock up even more. *I do hope my mate finds what he's looking for in those papers before he flakes out on me.*

Chapter Seventeen

Rowan hadn't been so wired since he was studying for his final exams at college. Sleep was impossible. His skin was so sensitive he felt a jolt every time Shadow brushed against him. He was almost relieved when Shadow got called downstairs to greet even more friends of his from the army. At least now he didn't have to contend with wanting to sink his teeth into the man every five minutes. His wolf had gotten quite pushy about his mate since he'd shifted, and Rowan could only assume it was because of his near-death experience – at least that was what he was telling himself.

Reaching for his cup of coffee sitting on the bedside table, Rowan scowled when he saw it was empty and the pot beside it was just as dry. The bed was littered with papers – three years' worth of bank statements printed out, which Rowan was cross checking against his list of pack members.

"There's something off here, I freaking know there is," he muttered to himself as he checked the list again. For the most part, the figures added up. The pack member file wasn't just a list of names. It included the age, mated status of any couples, the number of children in the household, as well as income earnings for each person which was updated annually. The latest figures related to three months before.

Rowan shook his head. Even little Tommy Sanderson had been hit up for tithes when he took on a paper round earlier that year, which Rowan thought was shit considering the boy was only twelve. Tommy earned the princely sum of $18.40 a week, and $3.70 of that was taken for tithe. Rowan's own modest income was based on his highest earning month over the past year, at $1222.20. As he was paid royalties, there were some months when he was lucky if he made five hundred dollars, but his tithe was still $244.44 every single month, regardless of what went into his own bank account on a monthly basis.

Thank the Fates my lump sum from my game sale was being held in a trust until the game launches, Rowan thought with a sigh. With the release still two months away, he would have been stung for a huge amount of money in tithes if Percy caught wind of just how much that sale was worth. *If I'd been allowed to keep any of it at all.*

His eyes flicked up the list and he frowned as it landed on a name he knew reasonably well. Melissa Joy, aged twenty-four, was listed with one dependent, her son Brandon who was three years old. Under Percy's tithe rule, she should have been paying forty percent of her $750 per month income. Rowan checked back on the bank statements. It was only showing $50 payments from her account instead of the $300 she should have been paying. Not only that, but Rowan knew she had a partner living with her. He'd seen the guy on Melissa's stoop one morning and his grandmother confirmed Melissa was mated now and had been for some time.

But mated to who? There was no partner name against Melissa's family, although she was listed as mated. Rowan glanced over at the clock, keen to call his grandmother and ask. But the digits showed it was after two in the morning and she would be asleep. *Just like I should be,* Rowan thought as he rubbed his eyes and winced as they stung. *What the fuck is taking Shadow so long? Those men must be gossiping like old women.*

Picking up his pen, he made a notation against Melissa's name and started looking through the pack list with a more critical eye. Percy wasn't known for cutting anyone any slack when it came to tithe payments. Maybe there were other "special cases," Shadow would want to know about.

/~/~/~/~/

Leaning back in his chair, Shadow rested the edge of his foot on the kitchen table, a beer in his hand and a smile on his face. Bernie was busy telling a tall tale that involved two red heads and a pissed off captain, while Rutig was egging him on. Dominic, Marco and Craven were similarly relaxed with the remains of their meal still cluttering the table. The scene reminded Shadow of the years spent in the army. The six wolf shifters had gravitated to each other during Shadow's first deployment and they'd been solid friends ever since.

He chuckled as Bernie yelled, "she held out her beer bottle and said 'stick it in that'. I mean, I said, 'what the hell darling, if you think any dick will fit down the neck of that, you've been deprived your whole life'. Total crack up, I tell you. Rutig was in the process of pulling out his dick, to prove my point you understand, when we got thrown out."

"It's good to have supportive friends." Shadow waved his beer in salute as the others laughed.

"So," Rutig said, nursing his own beer. A beta wolf, Rutig had muscles on top of muscles, but his dark eyes were as sharp as they ever were, regardless of the number of empty bottles scattered across the tables. "By my reckoning, we're one short in our band of merry men this evening. Don't tell me curly-locks refused your claim."

"Rowan's resting, in *our* bed," Shadow said more sharply than he intended. "He was kidnapped, badly injured, and rescued all in the past twenty-four hours, in case you forgot. You can both meet him in the morning when you cook us all breakfast."

"And you're down here, talking to us, instead of in bed with that little hottie?" Rutig rubbed behind his ear as he shook his head. "Man, Shadow, you've changed. Shit, when you showed us that little cutie's graduation photo, I was ready to hop on a plane and get over here and claim him before you did. A sweet omega wolf, with no need to prep him beyond a finger or two. Fuck man, I wish I could be so lucky."

Shadow snarled as Bernie slapped his friend around the head, hard. "Cut it out, Rut. That's not how mates are meant to be talked about. You'll see for yourself when you find your own. Now zip it."

Leaning his elbows on the table, Craven said quietly, "Our illustrious alpha has had a few teething problems with his mating, but a lot of that has to do with the state of this pack. Shadow can't be expected to woo his mate and weed out the troubles here all at the same time. This is not the home sweet home Shadow used to talk about, and Rowan is..." Craven bit his lip, looking at Shadow.

"Rowan was hurt, and I don't just mean today," Shadow said, grateful for Craven's discretion, but keen for his friends to understand the true depth of the situation. "My brother beat him badly, and I think that's why Rowan's gran got in touch with me although she never said specifically. He walks with a limp. It's permanent."

The silence was respectful. It was Bernie who spoke up first. "I guess that means we're all going to have to be on our A-game then, doesn't it? If there are shits in this pack, then we clean them out. No omega deserves to be abused by the people who're supposed to protect them."

"There might not be many pack members left by the time we're finished," Dominic said, opening another beer. "The elders are as corrupt as hell. Shadow's brother and his cronies are dead, but it doesn't seem to have made much difference. The only people who've tried to do something positive to help are a guy called Harry who lost his son to drugs, Talon, and Rowan's gran. Personally, I'm all for getting a bulldozer and trashing the whole fucking place. Gives me the heebie-jeebies wandering around here and everyone slinking in the shadows, freaking gossiping among themselves. But they don't speak to us or tell us what's wrong so we can fix it."

Shadow felt much the same way. It would be so easy to walk away with Rowan tucked under his arm. But he wasn't about to quit just yet. There was still Rowan's gran to consider, if nothing else. He wasn't about to leave her on her own. "We've been playing nice with them so far, maybe now..." He stopped as Rowan came hobbling into the room, brandishing a stack of papers. His sleep pants were dropping dangerously low over his ass, and the moment his sweet scent hit Shadow's nose, Shadow's cock stood up and saluted.

"I found something, I found something," Rowan said excitedly, waving his papers about. And then, he must have realized there were two strangers in the room, and he stopped, his eyes wide. His papers slapped against his bare chest as he tried to cover himself. "Er... Er..."

"Little red, I thought you'd be sleeping by now. You've caught us doing what all good army buddies do best. Gossiping." Shadow smiled as he dropped his foot from the table back on the floor and patted his thigh. "Come and sit with me. These two new guys are Bernie and Rutig. Bernie's the guy with the nose stud and earing, Rutig is known for his muscles. But they're good guys. You can trust them."

"Nice to meet you." Rowan bobbed his head as he sidled around the table to where Shadow was sitting. "I didn't think," he said quietly as he edged his ass on Shadow's thigh. "Haven't you guys been traveling all day?"

"Bernie barely let me stop for a piss break," Rutig said with a yawn. "Don't worry about us. We'll crash when we've heard your news. Shadow and the others have already filled us in on most of what's going on."

Shadow bit his lip to stop from groaning as his fingers encountered Rowan's naked belly. *It's just to stop him falling off my lap,* he told himself as he pulled his mate close. *Rutig was right. I am so damn lucky.*

Rowan looked up at him, his green eyes sparkling although they were lined with red. "I think I've found our problem," he said shyly. "I'm fairly sure the pack's been infiltrated. We've got spies in our territory."

Chapter Eighteen

It turned out the men were more receptive to what Rowan explained than he thought they'd be. It helped that Dominic, who Rowan was starting to see as the brains among his friends, had taken an inventory of who was living in the houses they'd visited as part of the alpha meet and greet done just after the pack meeting. By cross checking Dominic's list against the established pack record, they quickly found five families who had "extra" family members not on the pack list. In each of those cases Rowan had already flagged the family because their tithe amounts were considerably lower than they should have been.

"What the fuck is going on with this damn pack?" Shadow groaned, shoving the papers away from him and leaning back in his chair.

Rowan had stayed perched on his lap and wondered if he should get off. His mate looked exhausted and out of the window, he could see the first blush of daybreak. He was just about to suggest they all get some sleep, when Craven asked, "What's the pack policy about non-pack members visiting the territory?"

"I don't see how that matters," Bernie said with a yawn. "Maybe this is just a case of some of the families here being close buddies with Percy and getting reduced tithes and special privileges because of it."

"No, no, Craven's got a good point," Rowan said quickly. "This pack never allows non-pack members to stay in the territory overnight. Even visiting members from other packs had to stay in hotels over on the human side of town if they were here for more than a day. I remember specifically, because Gran got real upset when her friend Sandy had a cousin come over from England. The woman was planning to stay for a week, but Percy wouldn't give her permission to stay in a pack-owned house, so she had to cut her trip short. The hotel fees were more than she'd budgeted for on her trip. Sandy was gutted and wanted to leave the pack, but her husband said she couldn't take the kids if she did."

"Sandy and her husband aren't true mates, are they?" Shadow asked.

"No. Very few couples in this pack are," Rowan said with a sigh. "I mean, no one really gets the chance to interact with anyone other than the humans they might work with and non-pack members aren't encouraged to visit this territory either. The big parties over on Rogue Alley were the only times anyone could wander around here, and that was all so Percy could sell his drugs."

"This place sounds more like a cult than a pack every day," Marco said covering his yawn. The men were all showing signs of exhaustion. "Our problem is going to be fucking manpower. We're going to have to hit all these five families at the same time, otherwise we're going to lose some of them and it's clear whoever's behind all of this is too scared to show his fucking face."

"And we still haven't worked out where my late brother was getting his drugs from in the first place," Shadow snapped. "I half expect some heavy to turn up, pounding on the door and demanding money because Percy stiffed him for his cut or something."

"They'd be banging on some door in Rogue Alley," Rowan said quietly. "I told you, Percy never allowed anyone in this house."

"And from the state of this place, it's not surprising." Dominic grabbed some of the empties off the table and stood up. "We can talk forever and still not get anywhere. I say we sleep in shifts – two hours rotation guarding the house, then bed. Reconvene at six tonight and go and drag in five more families for a fucking interrogation. Craven and I can take first guard shift, then Marco and Shadow. You and Rutig can take the last shift, Bernie, seeing as you guys haven't slept since you got here and by then me and Craven should be awake."

"I can't leave the elders sitting down in the cells for too long or I'll have a riot on my hands," Shadow said firmly. "You five work out the guard duty among yourselves and make sure all of you get some sleep. Call in Harry and Talon if you need to. They'll both be awake soon. I'm going to get my sweet mate tucked up in bed, and then I'm going to pull Simon out of his cell and start interrogating him."

"You are not doing that without me." Rowan was gutted. He really thought he'd done something positive for his mate, finding out about the interlopers and the reduced tithe payments. He was stung to the core Shadow thought he should stay in bed when there was still work to be done.

The hands resting around his waist firmed against his skin. "Little red," Shadow crooned in that low sexy voice that made Rowan's insides melt and his cock perk up despite how tired he was. "I'm not saying you can't be there, babe. It's just you're going to need your sleep when I'm done putting you to bed." His cocky grin was guaranteed to make a man drop his pants.

"Seriously?" Rowan jumped off Shadow's lap, grabbing at the waist band of his sleep pants as they threatened to fall off. He turned to his mate and fixed him with his best glare. "You're planning to sex me up to shut me up, so you can go and rough up that sleazy elder while I'm sleeping apparently being tired out from all your alpha attentions? What the hell were you thinking, saying something like that?"

Someone laughed, but Rowan only had eyes for his mate. Was he blushing? *If he isn't, he damn should be. Treating me like a concubine.*

"I didn't mean it quite like that," Shadow said quickly, reaching out as if to pull him close again. When Rowan evaded his grabby hands, Shadow pouted. He actually pouted like a teenager and Rowan would have laughed, but he was too pissed off.

"That's how it came across. Maybe you need to work on your delivery.

I'm going to get some clothes on," he said, sticking his nose in the air. "There'd better be fresh coffee made for me by the time I get back, and if you go near any of those prisoners before I'm ready, you'll be sleeping on the couch for a month. Alone!" he added for emphasis as he stomped out of the kitchen.

Stalking through the house as best he could with his leg aching, Rowan fumed. He was tired. He was so damn tired he could barely see straight, but he'd been just as exhausted before and pulled through it. If those rugged muscle-men with their buzz cuts thought he needed to be tucked up in bed while they did all the heavy work, they had a lot to learn about their alpha mate.

Damn alpha, trying to use his alpha hormones to side line me, Rowan continued his inner rant as he grabbed his clothes. He wouldn't have minded so much – it was heady being seen as sexually desirable by such a strong male – but his damned mate used their natural attraction to each other to achieve his own ends.

Shadow was just as tired as he was. Rowan had seen that in the dark smudges under his mate's eyes and the weary slump of his shoulders. There was a tiny part of him that felt guilty for adding more stress to his mate's shoulders, but he shoved that feeling aside. The one thing he had decided for himself, while he was trapped in that water tower was if he got out, he was going to meet life head on, and that included the problems his pack was having. He'd thought, after the talk Shadow and he shared, that his mate agreed, but clearly that was a five minute aberration spoken in the heat of a moment that didn't last.

Buttoning up his shirt, Rowan pushed his sleep pants off his hips and left them on the floor. He sat on the edge of the bed, his back aching as he bent over to tug a pair of jeans over his feet. The scars on his bad leg were red and angry looking, and he rubbed over them, willing the aches away.

The mattress under his butt was so soft and all Rowan wanted to do was lie back and ignore the world for at least ten hours. But he couldn't do it. *I have to get my mate to see me as an equal in this relationship or it's never going to work.* And that meant ignoring his tiredness, just as Shadow was doing and forging onwards. Pulling his jeans up, Rowan stood so he could get the material over his bare ass, zipping up quickly. *Jacket or no jacket?* It wasn't that cold in the house, but Rowan found the one he wore when he was interviewed for his degree and shrugged it over his shoulders.

He caught sight of himself in the mirror. His curls were all over the place, but the rest of him looked clean and casually smart. He straightened his back and gave himself a nod. "I'm definitely alpha mate material," he told his reflection, "and I'll kick anyone who tries to suggest otherwise." Which reminded him. Rowan found his boots and slipped them on. *Now, I just need coffee,* he thought as he tried to keep his balance even as he walked out to find Shadow.

Chapter Nineteen

Shadow knew he'd fucked up big time with his mate and he wasn't sure the large mug of coffee he'd prepared would qualify as an apology. He imagined Rowan would have more to say to him, as he hovered at the foot of the stairs, but his mate just accepted the coffee he offered and took a long sip, before saying, "Shall we get this over with?"

"This could get ugly," Shadow warned in a low voice as he led his mate towards the basement door. The padlock was already open, the hinges creaking as he swung the door wide. "Simon was terrified when I hassled him about your whereabouts. He could do something stupid."

"Stupid is his middle name," Rowan said curtly. "Don't hold back from tearing his throat out on my account. I'm too tired to give a damn."

Which is why you should be in bed. But then, Shadow knew they both should be. The army had trained him to go without sleep for days, but the previous twenty-four hours had been an emotional tornado. The only thing burning in Shadow's mind was the desire to know the name and nature of the danger that was threatening his pack and then he wanted some serious time to grovel to his mate.

He nodded at Marco who was standing outside the interview room. "I put him in here," Marco said gruffly. "Talon's awake, and Harry's on his way over. They're both going on guard duty while the others get some shut eye. I'll stay out here and watch that none of the other elders get mouthy, until you're done. Simon's yells woke them up."

Shadow could've hugged his intuitive friend. Marco was well aware Shadow could hold his own against any wolf, but the same couldn't be said for the alpha mate and moving Simon to the interview room meant at least his mate could sit down. He nodded instead, opening the door and striding inside, feeling Rowan's presence behind him. The door slammed with a clunk.

The room was bare except for a small wooden table that was listing on one side, and four straight-backed chairs. Simon was sitting in one of them, a glower on his face that was marred by a huge red mark about the size of Marco's fist. Shadow inwardly smirked. Marco had never been known for his diplomacy skills, especially at five in the morning.

Dragging a chair away from the table for Rowan to sit on, Shadow stayed standing, his face expressionless. He'd often used silence as an interrogation tool, especially with someone as weak willed as the man in front of him. But it seemed his mate had other ideas. Sitting down and taking a long sip of his coffee, Rowan said brightly, "I hear you had me kidnapped and were planning to give me to some mastermind who's threatening my mate and the pack. Want to tell me what that's about?"

"I don't have to say anything to you," Simon turned his focus on Rowan and snarled. Shadow was ready to beat him then and there, but it seemed Rowan wasn't finished.

"That's true," he said in the same bright tone. "You don't have to say anything despite the fact I am this pack's alpha mate, Simon. I mean, it's not as though you're going to be allowed to stay with the pack, that's if you're still breathing when this interview is over. Shadow's pretty mad about the whole water tower incident, and frankly, I rank your chances of getting out of here alive at about twenty percent at best. Of course, that ranking is subject to change but that depends entirely on anything you may or may not say. It's up to you."

Shadow watched Simon's eyes flicker between Rowan and himself. *Yeah, you know who the bigger threat is, asshole,* he thought, although he made sure his expression didn't change. Rowan was still sipping his coffee, watching Simon as if he was a curiosity.

"I'm not saying anything." Simon folded his arms across his chest.

Rowan shrugged. Shadow didn't move. After a few long moments, Simon started to fidget.

"He'll know, you know," Simon said at last. "This guy you're up against has been determined to get this pack one way or another for years. He only let Percy stick around and act like he's the boss because he knew you'd come out of the woodwork eventually. I mean, there's no point in killing a beta son, if an alpha son is still in the wings, is there?"

"Oh, we know all about him," Rowan said airily as if he and Simon were just gossiping about the weather. "We've already traced the other members of his rogue gang. No, no, all we want to know is about the drugs. Why does this guy of yours want a pack full of druggies? I mean, if everyone is under the influence it's not as though they can fight, work, or do anything positive for the alpha or the rest of the pack. Look at Harry's son for example. He was one of the fittest wolves I knew, and he died from using drugs."

Smart mate, Shadow thought approvingly. Rowan hadn't actually lied, something that could be scented by any paranormal if he did. He also admired the fact that Rowan was talking to Simon, with just the right amount of omega concern. *It's remarkably effective.*

"That boy wasn't meant to die. That was all Percy's doing," Simon lifted the corner of his lip. "The drugs Percy was peddling were all human based. Bart resisted... resisted big time and didn't want a bar of Percy or what he was doing. He became a challenge and when Percy told Bart the drugs were for humans and wouldn't even impact them, he dared Bart to try it. The poor sod didn't know it was laced. By the time he did, it was already too late. Percy crowed about it for weeks and held the whole thing over our heads, showing us what would happen if we crossed him."

"It was a shame. Bart was a nice guy," Rowan agreed. "He definitely didn't deserve to die like that, but then drugs will fuck up anyone, users and sellers alike. It's weird though, don't you think? I mean you're an elder. Have you ever seen any pack be interested in drug distribution before? I just can't see the point myself."

Shadow was stunned. While he was struggling with the urge to rip Simon a new asshole, Rowan was chatting to him like the trusted advisor Simon was supposed to be. The skill, that ability to talk to a person and make them feel as though they were the only person of importance, was amazing. And Simon was lapping it up.

"We've become infected by a consumer-based society, always wanting more, more, more." Simon leaned his elbows on the table, his defensive posture from before completely gone. "Wolves of old never bothered about such things. But then, they didn't live and work among humans either. They had their hierarchy, every wolf knew what was expected of them, they lived off the land, and all looked after each other."

"I see," Rowan nodded eagerly. "So, this whole drug dealing proposition is like a revenge thing. I mean, humans took over the lands we used to run free on, decimated our hunting grounds, built cities in the huge tracts of forest we used to live on, and shifters had no choice but to assimilate or die."

"Exactly." Simon slammed his open palm on the table. "I mean, I wasn't keen on the idea at first. But I remember when this pack was completely surrounded by land, streams, and forests. The odd human came around and he was either avoided or gently persuaded to leave. But then the rail line came through. Honestly, it was like you blinked and there was a fucking town where our lands used to be. And there was nothing we could do. The old alpha back then – Percy's grandfather – he tried to stop the progress, but we didn't know about land ownership or things like that. We were lucky to keep a hold of the houses we did have."

"Buying land costs so much money," Rowan sighed and looked suitably compassionate. "I noticed that in college. Honestly, if there was any demand for housing at all, the prices all seemed to sky rocket."

"And that's exactly what happened here. You're too young to remember, omega." Simon seemed to have forgotten Shadow was even in the room, which was further testament to Rowan's interviewing skills. "But Percy's father didn't help. He was content to sit on the land his father had managed to buy and do nothing. He said we all had enough, but that's not how a wolf is supposed to live. We were born to wander, to spread out, hunt and procreate the way nature intended. Davos approached the old alpha when Gray left, asking to be admitted to the pack and telling the alpha what could be done to change everything, but the damn man wouldn't listen. In the meantime, the pack were working for humans, living on minimum wages."

"It's not a bad plan in theory," Rowan agreed, while Shadow barely dared to breathe. The spell Rowan was weaving was tightening. "You can see how it would work. It's a two-fold effect. On the one hand, pack members selling drugs make more money so they can afford to buy up more houses and move the humans out. On the other hand, you've got addicted humans who can't meet their mortgages, so their houses come up for sale through the banks and can be bought for pennies on the dollar. It's not as though wolf shifters are affected by street drugs anyway."

"I always knew you were smarter than you looked, omega," Simon nodded vigorously. "Percy didn't get it – he thought the only way to make the pack do what he wanted was to starve them or beat them into submission. He couldn't sell the big idea because he didn't understand it, and boy, Davos was pissed off about that. You know if Gray hadn't have killed that menace the way he did, Davos was going to do it anyway."

"That would have made things awkward though, wouldn't it?" Rowan tilted his head slightly to one side. "I mean, the old alpha is still alive, and it's not as though anyone gets any honor from challenging him with him being off his rocker the way he is. I guess that's why Davos put more of his people in the pack? So, that he'd have more support when the time came for Davos to take over."

"That's part of it, yes. Davos needed to know he had an inner circle already in place who knew the workings of the pack. Clinton's due back next week, and from what Davos said, that shipment will be the biggest yet. Getting new people to help distribute it is going to be an issue if things don't change though."

Shadow could see Simon totally believed what he was saying. He genuinely thought the pack's resistance to selling drugs was an issue.

"Oh, my gods," Rowan squealed and clapped his hands. "So that's why you elders all took so many holidays overseas. That is so clever, and with the police already in Davos' back pocket, no one will suspect a thing."

Simon actually preened. "It was my idea," he said with a smile. "There was no point in buying drugs from human thugs who lived in neighboring towns. That's just inviting them to come in and take a piece of the action. Every single drug sold within a fifty-mile radius comes from us. If someone does try and muscle in, then Davos' crew kicks them out and sends a warning to them never to come back."

"Davos really did think he had everything covered and he was damned close." Rowan finished his coffee and stood up, heading for the door, pausing as he looked back. "As nice as it has been talking to you Simon, I truly think you've had too much European sun and it's addled your brain."

Simon's mouth dropped open and his eyes widened.

"The fact of the matter is, one of the enduring legacies of a wolf shifter is their honor, their need to protect pack and family, and to ensure that every pack member lives a life free from coercion and abuse. I'm not saying Percy's grandfather did the right thing in ignoring the human development around his territory; that is something that can't be undone. But encouraging the high tithes that have crippled this pack; turning a blind eye to the abuses Percy and his cronies inflicted on the weaker members who rely on their alpha to protect them. Those actions are all on you and your fellow elders, Simon. You did this. You allowed a rogue wolf, who should have been reported to the council the first time he set foot on this territory, to muscle their way in and tear this pack apart."

"I thought you agreed with Davos' ideas, could understand his vision," Simon spluttered.

"I said I could see how the ideas could work in theory," Rowan said. "But revenge is never the answer and rogue wolves are so named for a reason. You will be held responsible for your part in all of this, as will the rest of the elders in this pack. You personally will have to answer for your crimes of facilitating the abduction and illegal holding of the pack's alpha mate and one of the inner circle. And I happen to know that the new alpha of this pack is someone with a high standard of honor, who has had a lot of experience with meting out justice in the wolf tradition."

"I can help you." Simon's face was bright red and he finally turned his attention on Shadow. "I can tell you everything, show you where the drugs are coming in, where they are being held, who the contacts are in the police. Everything."

Shadow flicked a glance at his mate.

Rowan smiled. "We don't need him. We have the name we were looking for; we know how the drugs are getting in and we know why Davos wanted this pack. By six o'clock tonight the elders will all be in council hands, Federal Customs officers will be alerted on Clinton's return, and the interlopers who work with Davos will be in shifter council jail where they belong. If Davos makes a move after that, he will be dealt with, just as surely as you will be now. Simon, your chances of getting out of this room alive, have just dropped down to zero."

Rowan opened the door, holding it wide for Marco to come inside. "I'll leave you gentlemen to it. I'll be in bed when you're looking for me, Alpha," he said, his smile widening as he sauntered out of the door.

"That is one amazing fucking omega," Marco said as he slammed the door shut behind the alpha mate. "Ready to shift, Alpha? Or are you just going to give him an old-fashioned pounding?"

"I'll shift." Shadow flexed his fingers that were already showing as claws and attacked the opening of his pants. He glared at Simon as he pushed his pants down his legs. "I'd give anything to drag this out and make you suffer the way you hurt my poor Rowan, but you heard what he said. He's waiting for me, in bed, as true, as loyal, and as sweet as any alpha mate should be. I'd far rather hear his screams of passion than listen to you whimper and beg for your pathetic life. You're honestly not worth the hassle."

Kicking his pants off, Shadow shifted, every ounce of his anger and frustration over Rowan's abduction coming to the fore. His wolf was totally on board with Shadow's assessment of the situation. Justice was swift and only a little bit messy. Still in his four-legged form, Shadow howled his victory as Marco let him out of the interview room. From all around the pack house, he heard the howls of his friends celebrating with him.

/~/~/~/~/

Up in the room they shared, Rowan heard the howls and closed his eyes, praying to the Fates that Simon's justice was quick. Simon's frustration over the encroachment of humans on their land could be understood, but Rowan had learned in college that

263

many humans wanted exactly the same things as a wolf shifter did – a safe roof over their head, a love to hold them through the dark times, and the ability to put food on the table for their families.

Simon and the other elders had turned away from the core family values that wolves enshrined. *Maybe, if the Fates grant him another life, he'll find his true mate, and lead the life he should've done this time.* Rowan made a note on his phone to contact Simon's widow and make sure there was a pack pension plan in place to take care of her and the children. He smiled as he did it. *Look at me, being all alpha-matey.*

Putting the phone on the bedside cabinet, Rowan crawled into bed, groaning as his muscles relaxed into the mattress. Daylight peered around the corner of the curtains, and Rowan was glad he'd thought to get rid of his food and papers off the bed before he'd gone down to the kitchen earlier.

I should wait for Shadow, he thought as he closed his eyes. *I still have a bone to pick with him.* But even as he thought it, his brain shut down. Within seconds he was asleep.

Chapter Twenty

Shadow yawned and stretched out one arm, his eyes opening to long afternoon shadows coming from the windows. He had no idea how long he'd slept, but his sweet mate was still curled up on his other arm, his soft breath wafting across his bicep with every exhale. *He's so beautiful,* Shadow forced himself to take stock, slow down and really look at the man he'd claimed.

It'd been another two hours after Simon's death, before Shadow made it to bed. The elder's screaming and his personal victorious howl set off the other prisoners, and he was forced to deal with them, then and there. Dominic, who hadn't gone to bed with the others, talked to the shifter council while Shadow interrogated the remaining elders. They'd been charged with stealing from the pack, interfering in human affairs and giving aid and comfort to rogues. The council was quick to pick them up and Shadow knew they'd be in for more grilling about Davos' whereabouts.

The three teenagers were terrified, and suitably subdued after a night in the cells. While Shadow found it difficult to forgive them for what they'd done to Rowan and Talon, he did his best to be fair. Talon growling in the corner of the room and flicking his knives while Shadow interviewed them reinforced his assertions that the three members would not get another chance. Telling them firmly, along with a strong dose of alpha power, to use commonsense, or at least talk to their parents before they did something stupid again was the best he could do with those three.

Leaving Craven and Dominic to handle the council who'd responded to the news about Clinton's drug shipments – they promised they'd liaise with the federal authorities, Shadow finally made it to bed while the others were enjoying morning tea. He hadn't expected Rowan to be awake, and he also hadn't expected the jolt in his heart when he saw his sweet mate sleeping. He looked so innocent. After fighting and killing, Shadow's wolf desperately wanted to cement his claim on their alpha mate, but Rowan was so adorable in his sleep, Shadow didn't have the heart to wake him.

Besides, Shadow also knew he had to do right by his mate this time, or he'd be living on hand and blow jobs for the rest of their natural lives. While they were extremely enjoyable, Shadow would never forget the sheer exhilaration he felt, the first, and so far, only time he'd sunk his cock into Rowan's ass. *Something that special should be treasured*, he thought as he gently lifted the covers, taking in Rowan's sleek body.

Rowan was lying on his front, his scarred leg sprawled out and bent at the knee, accentuating the sweet curve of his ass. His scent unmasked now the covers were lifted, called to every primitive instinct Shadow had. But he forced himself to remember the shame and embarrassment he felt ruining his virginal mate's first time.

Rowan snuffled and wiggled. Shadow pulled the covers back over the tempting body, trying to come up with a gentle plan of attack. His wolf's, and cock's, instincts were all for plowing the sweet hole he'd just caught a glimpse of, *but that's not going to work this time,* he reminded himself firmly.

Sex with hook ups were so easy. Both men knew what they wanted – relief for an aching cock. Simple. Shadow and his friends didn't even have to work for it. Their uniform and military bearing, combined with shifter genetics, meant men quite literally fell all over them anytime they went on the prowl.

Rowan didn't.

Sure, Shadow knew he was attractive to his mate. Rowan's pants plumped out frequently when he was around, but he was also skittish, as if knowing if he gave Shadow the slightest bit of encouragement, Shadow would be over him like a rash and plowing him like a piston. *Oh, my gods, and I would be too, in a freaking heartbeat.* Shadow muffled his groan. *Think man, think. Think with something other than your cock.*

He tried to remember what was on Rowan's list. Kissing. He remembered that and Rowan did seem to enjoy that sort of thing. Exploring – Shadow would definitely allow his mate to do that when they had more than five minutes peace together, *But not today please.* Shadow was sure his balls were going to burst if he didn't get relief soon.

Okay. F-o-r-e-p-l-a-y. Shadow studied the play of light on the ceiling. Clearly the word foreplay denoted something more than a quick slurp of a guy's cock before lubing up his fingers. *Duh.* Shadow would have slapped himself, but he didn't want to wake his mate just yet, but damn, he'd just remembered, that Rowan as an omega, would self-lube and be ready for him, if he was properly aroused. That was how it worked between alpha and omega true mate pairings.

I've got to draw this out, so Rowan's body has time to adjust. I need him begging for it. Shadow's grin was probably evil, but it wasn't as though anyone was watching him. *Think ROMANCE,* he told himself firmly, and then he remembered. A long hot dusty night a few years before. He and the guys were in the hall, there was a movie playing. There was very little action in it. Shadow and his friends were sitting at the back, muttering between themselves because they were bored.

The storyline was supposed to be a comedy, although Shadow didn't remember laughing. But he did remember the sex scene. A man and a woman, a lot of gasping going on which all sounded fake to him. But he did recall how the woman seemed to respond to the caresses and the kisses all over her body.

Rowan was definitely not a woman, but that didn't mean he couldn't appreciate the softer side of loving.

Shadow scrunched his eyes shut, struggling with his control as his mate wiggled closer, brushing his ass against Shadow's thigh. *KISS HIM,* his wolf and cock yelled at him. *Kiss him all over if you have to, but for gods sake don't just lay there like a lump hoping he'll jump on and ride you till you're drained.*

Slow touches. Shadow rolled back towards his mate, raining butterfly kisses across Rowan's back and neck. He nuzzled his nose in his mate's bright red curls, inhaling deeply as his hand drifted slowly up and down the side of Rowan's torso. *Hmm, this is nice,* he thought, making sure to keep his hips firmly away from the heat of Rowan's skin.

Rowan murmured something nonsensical, tilting his head and arching his neck, so Shadow kissed down the gentle arch, and nibbled on the mating scar he'd left. He let his hand scoot around his mate's chest, stroking the skin, flicking the wee nipples that beaded under his fingers. Rowan moaned and stretched out, offering more of his body up to Shadow's fingers.

With a gentle push, Shadow rolled Rowan onto his back and loomed over him, his lips never leaving the warm skin as they trailed over Rowan's sharp collar bone, first one side and then the other. Rowan's cock was already firm, and his mate wriggled his hips restlessly, but Shadow made sure he didn't press his body on his mate's lower half.

Instead, he moved his head, backwards and forwards over Rowan's torso, taking in his mate's unique taste and scent through his tongue. *Oh, I could eat you up so badly,* he thought, letting his groan play across Rowan's skin. He trailed his fingers up the sides of Rowan's body, under the arm, and across the slender biceps before heading back down again. His mate's body was limp, relaxed and the small moans were music to Shadow's ears.

Slowly, take it slow. Shadow moved his head further down, trailing his tongue over Rowan's soft belly. His mate's cock was slender, leaving dribbles on his chin where it nudged him. But Shadow ignored it for now, as he left a series of small nips down the sharp V caused by Rowan's hip bones.

"Oh, my gods, Shadow." Rowan's voice was a whisper, but the hands that landed on his head were firm. There was no pushing involved. Shadow doubted an omega wolf could ever be sexually aggressive. But when he ran his nose down the join where leg met groin, Rowan spread his legs wider, his hips jolting upwards as his cock sought the friction it needed.

Shadow could smell it. His omega's juices hitting the air, a signal to his mate that his body was prepping itself. But instead of diving in, like he'd done the time before, Shadow licked over Rowan's balls, feeling them move under his tightening ball sack. The small indent, right where the two balls sat at the base of Rowan's length was saturated in scent. Strong, potent, designed to drive alphas wild, and Shadow was pushing back against his instincts.

He'd never tasted Rowan's cock. Rowan was learning how to please him with his mouth, but any time he had, Shadow had finished his mate off with his hand. It wasn't that he didn't enjoy oral, it'd just never worked out that way so far. But when Shadow enclosed his mouth over the angry red tip of Rowan's cock, he silently vowed he'd be doing it again. Beads of Rowan's precome coated his tongue, and Shadow moved, so he could tilt his neck better to take more of the cock inside.

Better than steak, Shadow thought as he sucked up, letting his lips and tongue play with the underside of Rowan's cock head. Rowan moaned, and groaned, and the hands resting on Shadow's head flexed, his hips doing all they could to chase the sensations Shadow was causing.

My mate is delicious. Shadow hummed around the silken skin, bobbing his head up and down in slow movements, his broad tongue adding more sensations to the sensitive shaft. Rowan's legs were spread wide, his stuttering hip movements nothing Shadow couldn't handle.

The more Shadow sucked, the more vocal Rowan became, and Shadow realized this was his mate's first ever blow job. Filled with pride at bringing Rowan so much pleasure, Shadow inhaled through his nose, and sunk his mouth down until his nose brushed against his mate's groin. One well timed swallow, and Rowan yelled out as Shadow pulled back far enough to taste his mate's spunk on his tongue. *That's everything awesome about a man right there,* Shadow thought happily as he used his tongue to keep Rowan's cock firm.

"Shadow... Shadow... Can you... I feel..." Rowan was panting hard, his cheeks almost as red as his curls. A film of sweat coated his face, and his eyes were flashing wolf.

Slurping off Rowan's cock, Shadow grinned. *This is how it should've been last time.* Reaching down between Rowan's legs, he let his finger trail across that delicious tight skin between his balls and his hole. Keeping the bulk of his body off his mate, because *damn*, his cock was so heavy he could pole vault on it, Shadow rested his arm beside Rowan's head, leaning his head down so his mate could taste himself on Shadow's tongue.

Rowan's arms were strong around his neck, his whole body trembling. "Please... Need..." and Shadow felt the true depth of his mate's desire as his fingers slipped effortlessly into a drenched hole. *How could I have been so stupid to think he was ready last time? What a moron!* Keeping his mate focused with scorching kisses, Shadow increased the number of fingers he was using – two, three and then four. Fuck, with the way Rowan was writhing around, he was in danger of losing his fist.

"Please, please, please, please."

Shadow broke off the kissing, taking a well needed breath. Lost in his passion, Rowan had never looked so stunning and Shadow made a solemn silent promise that he'd bring that look to his mate's face every damn time.

"Are you sure you're ready?" Shadow had to ask, but damn it all to hell if Rowan flinched now, he'd cut his balls off and serve them to his mate for breakfast. Because Rowan owned him – it was that simple. Heart and soul, cock and balls, Rowan had it all, and if he didn't bring his mate pleasure this time, then Shadow was swearing off sex forever.

"I need you inside of me." No deceit, no concerns, just the sweet scent of Rowan's arousal filling the air. Removing his fingers, Shadow slathered the residue of Rowan's slick on his cock before reaching over Rowan's head for a pillow.

"This will make it easier for you," Shadow promised, tucking the pillow under Rowan's hips. He realized he was trembling; this was a first for Shadow too. He'd never been face to face with anyone he'd stuck his cock into before. Making sure there was absolutely no pressure on Rowan's bad leg, Shadow lined up, letting out a long breath as his mate's body accepted him easily.

There was a gasp, Shadow expected that. Rowan still wasn't used to anything inside of him. He slowed right down, rocking gently, his cock moving in infinitesimal increments, carefully opening his mate wide. Rowan's teeth were worrying his plump bottom lip, and Shadow leaned over, tenderly sucking the soft flesh away from the bite.

"Amazing," Rowan whispered, looping his arms around Shadow's neck. "Don't stop."

There was little fear of that. Shadow felt as though there was an iron band around his chest and groin – his visualization of control. But no matter how thick those iron bands might have been in his mind, they weren't going to hold him back forever. But the love he saw on Rowan's face managed to. Holding his mate's gaze, Shadow bottomed out, mentally counted to ten and slowly pulled almost all the way out again.

In and out, keeping things slow. Rowan's hands alternated by gripping and then soothing Shadow's nape. It was almost scary, and Shadow wasn't afraid of much, but every breath, every movement no matter how slight was so intense. Shadow could feel their bond strengthening and his heart expanding with every thrust. Rowan's facial expression was so open, showing everything his mate was feeling. The arousal was just part of it. Love was definitely there, but what struck Shadow most was the joy that lit Rowan's face from the inside, giving him a glow he'd never thought to dream of all those years they were apart.

They were moving totally in sync with each other. Shadow didn't even notice his thrusts had sped up, but Rowan was meeting him half way, his good leg, draped over the back of Shadow's thigh to anchor himself as he mirrored Shadow's movements. Shadow's fangs dropped. It wasn't intentional. Shadow hadn't even thought about biting his mate again. But Rowan sensed his need, tilting his neck so prettily making Shadow want to howl.

Pushing his hips just a tiny bit faster, Shadow leaned down, placing his lips over Rowan's original bite. *I love you little red,* he thought as his balls tightened to the point of no return and he bit down. Seconds later he felt an answering bite on the corner of his neck, and his whole body jolted as though he'd been hit with electricity. Every part of his body felt as though it was supercharged and in his mind's eye, he could see his rugged wolf spirit embracing Rowan's slighter white wolf form.

His balls throbbing, Shadow held still for the longest time. It was only when his arms started to tremble for a totally different reason this time, that he released his teeth, gently licking over the wound that remained. He felt the soft touch of his mate's tongue and he knew Rowan was doing the same.

"We can do that again, right?" Rowan's voice was hoarse as if he'd been screaming, but the brilliant emeralds of his eyes showed the true depth of how deeply and positively he felt. Then those same eyes looked shocked and Rowan opened his mouth to yell, just as Shadow felt a large thump on the back of his head.

Chapter Twenty-One

It took a lot to make Rowan really angry, but having some man in a mask, dressed in black, loom over their bed while his mate's cock was still inside of him was enough to do it. Unfortunately, he really wasn't in a position to do anything about it. He could only assume that the hormones and adrenalin that came from making love, Rowan was sure they did not just have sex, was the only reason Shadow hadn't flopped on top of him unconscious.

Something the intruder clearly hadn't factored into his plans. Rowan could see the whites of the man's eyes get wider as Shadow shook his head, grabbed the base of his cock and used as much care as possible to slide free. Rowan felt the gush of juices, his and his mate's, and was acutely aware of the cooling spunk on his belly, and now trickling down his ass cheeks. With his butt still propped up on the pillow and his legs spread wide, he'd never felt so vulnerable.

Not that he stayed that way for long. Ignoring the intruder for the moment, Shadow scooped up the covers, pushed away by their lovemaking, covering Rowan up to chest height before turning towards the man who'd so rudely interrupted them.

"What. The. Fuck. Do. You. Think. You're. Doing?" Each word clipped. Each word laden with menace. Naked, his cock still half hard, Shadow looked magnificent in his fury. Rowan couldn't help but be impressed.

"Hey, man," the intruder backed up towards the dresser. The tight clothes he was wearing indicated he was big, and had some muscle tone, but even naked, Shadow was far more imposing. "At least I let you finish."

"I'm supposed to be thankful for that?" Shadow's voice deepened into a growl. "You break in here, intruding on a private, intimate moment between me and my *true mate*, and you suggest I should be grateful you let my balls empty before you tried your pathetic attempt at knocking me out?"

"True mate? Fuck it." The intruder flicked his fingers as if trying to ward Shadow off. "That damn Elder was right about that. I told him I didn't believe it, what with you being in the military and all. Felt for sure you'd be knocking boots with the pack females the moment you got home, just like your brother used to do. Shit and damn, can nothing go to plan?"

Rowan's eyes widened. "You're Davos, the rogue who's trying to tear this pack apart." Clutching the covers to his chest, he wiggled up the bed, resting his back on the headboard.

"And you're the geek omega Percy was waiting for a big pay day from. I told that damn boy to leave you alone until the money came through, but no, he had to get his jollies somewhere and he got most of them from hurting you. But then he couldn't stand the thought that you were his brother's intended. That boy had serious mental health issues, I can tell you."

Shadow's snarl reminded the intruder of the biggest threat in the room. The intruder sighed as if put out. "I guess there's no point in hiding myself, seeing as you know who I am and it's getting damn hot in this mask. I can't really talk to you with it on, anyway." Reaching under his neck, the intruder tugged the mask off his face, shaking out his long brown hair. "Phew, those things are a damn nuisance."

"Dave?" Shadow looked shocked to see the older man.

Rowan looked between Davos and Shadow. "You two know each other?"

"Dave was an old friend of my father's. I remember him being around the house from back when I was a toddler. They were always together – my father and him and at one point he was my dad's trusted advisor until he suddenly disappeared. My father never said what happened to him."

"Disappeared my ass," Davos/Dave sneered. "Your old man banished me, labelled me as a rogue with the council. I'm surprised you remember me at all, it was so long ago. Percy definitely didn't know who I was."

"Percy was a fool, but my father wasn't. What did you do?" Shadow clenched his fists and took a step closer to his father's old friend.

"Fuck," Davos looked up at the ceiling as he cursed. "Of course, you'd ask that. You're more like your old man than you care to admit, but seeing as we're going to be working together, I suppose you should know. It wasn't as though it was a big deal. I was trying to help your father reclaim some of the old land the pack had before the humans moved in. There was a house fire, some kid got hurt, it didn't kill him, but your old man lost his head at me, and banished me from the pack. Stupid fool. The plan worked, the people moved out within the week and the house went on the market for peanuts seeing as most of it had fallen down."

Rowan pulled his knees up to his chest, wrapping his arms around them and the covers. "You don't like humans." It wasn't a question, but Davos seemed to feel the need to answer anyway.

"Don't go getting judgmental with me just because you went to college. I've got no reason to like humans. They took our land."

"Any human that came to town, bought up land that was available under the laws," Shadow said sharply. "They didn't take anything; they bought their homes with hard earned money. Just because the wolves back at that time didn't realize the necessity of it, seeing as they just ran wild wherever they wanted to, didn't mean the humans were wrong in this. In the meantime, you caused dissent in this pack, encouraged Percy to strip the assets from the pack members so everyone here suffered, unless they were part of your plan. How do you justify doing any of that?"

"Some people need to suffer before they fall into line." Davos seemed genuinely shocked by Shadow's anger. "Alphas have to make the hard decisions."

"But you're not an alpha, and what have you achieved?" Shadow roared.

"Ten years I was gone. Percy was supposedly in charge for eight of those years. The pack kids are starving. Family bonds are strained to breaking point by the adults working two or more jobs just to put food on the table. Percy sold houses that had been in some families for generations. How is that helping anyone?"

"All they had to do was follow the new order," Davos said, his expression implying Shadow was stupid. Hugging his knees, Rowan kept his mouth shut. He wasn't going to help the idiot out of his current predicament.

"Whose new order? Yours?" Shadow demanded. "You don't have an alpha bone in your body, because if you had I'm sure you'd have challenged my father a decade ago and lost. Percy wasn't an alpha either. The only person who can lead a pack is a fucking alpha. And in this case, it's me!"

"Which is why I'm here," Davos said calmly. "I mean Percy didn't think about anything beyond how fast he could spend the cash in his hand. But you are a true alpha. You can make the people see..."

"See what?" Shadow snarled, closing the distance between him and Davos. Davos backed up until the dresser hit him in the back. "If I want evidence on how damn clever you are, I only have to look at what you did today."

"Today?" Davos' hand clutched at his throat. "Oh, you mean breaking in here. Yes, well, I had to, you see. Any other time you're always surrounded by other people."

"I was with my mate." Shadow loomed over him and Davos shrunk back, but he was stuck with nowhere to go.

"Yes, well, he wasn't any threat. Those other guys all looked like they would tear me apart before I had a chance to speak. That geek is just an omega..."

One swipe of Shadow's claws, and Davos started gurgling, blood welling up from the deep slash across his throat. Davos' hands were scrabbling, trying to stop the blood from flowing. Shadow grabbed him by his shirt and raised him off his feet. "I'm getting really fucking tired of people who don't listen to me," he growled as he shook the body and then dropped it on the floor. "Rowan isn't a geek or just an omega – he's the alpha mate!"

It was like time stopped for Rowan and Shadow, as they waited for Davos to die. Shadow was still magnificently naked, glaring at the hapless man ready to kill him all over again if he so much as twitched in the direction of the bed. Rowan rubbed the middle of his forehead as the sickly-sweet scent of blood infused the air.

"You know," he said quietly, when Davos finally stopped gurgling, "that blood is going to be hell to get out of the carpet."

"It always is," Shadow said glumly, looking down at the blood on his hands. "I'd better wash up and get some clothes on. I need to talk to the others and find out how the hell this bastard got in here in the first place."

"You can do that in a minute. Come here." Rowan held out his arms.

"But..." Shadow held up his stained hands.

"That doesn't matter. Come here."

Shadow slowly walked over to the bed. Rowan patted the space beside him. Sighing heavily, Shadow climbed up, careful not to touch anything with his hands. Rowan waited until they were sitting beside each other, then half-turned, and wrapped his arms around Shadow's waist, resting his head on Shadow's chest.

Shadow was stiff for a moment, but Rowan waited him out. Soon enough, his mate's arms wrapped around him, although Rowan noticed Shadow kept his hands away from his skin. "Now, isn't this nice?" Rowan said happily.

"There's a dead body wrecking the carpet, and my hands stink," Shadow said drily.

"Yes, well, we could do without that happening too often, but what we did before..." Rowan trailed off, looking up and meeting his mate's eyes. "I did hear you," he said quietly. "Just before you bit me, and filled my ass with all your delicious spunk, I heard what you were thinking."

Shadow was doing a great impersonation of a statue, the only thing moving was his eyes – looking to the left, looking to the right.

Rowan waited until those eyes were back on him again. "Did you mean it?"

Shadow hesitate, before saying softly, "With all that I am." His deep sincerity rang proud for Rowan to hear.

"That's great," Rowan said with a huge smile as he rested his head back on Shadow's chest. "Because I love you too, and now that Davos is gone, maybe we can work together to get this pack back on track again. After we've had dinner, of course."

"Of course. Anything else?" Rowan didn't have to look up to know Shadow was smiling.

"Well, we could probably do with a shower before we do anything else." Rowan allowed himself one more cuddle, then pushed himself off Shadow's chest and stretched. "I never did know if the omega prep mechanism works in water. Did you want to find out?"

Rowan laughed as Shadow scooped him off the bed and started running with him to the bathroom. His mate might not say much, and he wasn't one for hearts and flowers or romantic gestures. Shadow was a man of action, and that is exactly what Rowan loved about his huge alpha.

And yes, as Rowan found out later, his omega traits did manifest in the shower, and hearing the words "I love you" said out loud, was even more special when it was Shadow doing the talking.

Epilogue

Three months later

The hall was filled with light and laughter. It was Friday night and as was becoming a tradition for the pack now, all the members gathered for a potluck meal and a chance to catch up with their neighbors. Children ran among the tables under the watchful eyes of their parents. The smell of roast meats and grilling filled the air, and the chatter of people talking was lighthearted and jovial. At the head table, Shadow sat surrounded by his friends, leaning back in his chair with a beer in his hand.

Marco nudged him. "This is what we used to dream about. Do you remember?"

Shadow nodded. "Sitting in the desert, this type of thing was all I could dream about. Didn't think it would ever happen here," he admitted. "But then, I always thought my dad would be alive forever, and we'd be setting up something like this somewhere else."

"I could get used to this," Craven said with a happy sigh. "Happy people, sumptuous meals and being able to sleep in a comfortable bed every night. Makes a huge change from being on tours. I've been thinking it might be time to find a mate of my own, settle down, maybe have a kid or two to round out the picture."

"Don't go talking about mates just yet. You'll jinx us all," Rutig groaned. "I'll have you know that since I've started working at the local police department, I've come across some amazingly obliging humans who seem to enjoy my attentions. I don't want to disappoint any of them by finding my mate and pulling myself off the market. And I'm not getting any younger. I have to pace myself, you know."

"What, you're only seeing three people a night instead of five," Dominic laughed, and the others laughed with him.

That's what's different about this place, Shadow thought as he scanned the crowds for his beloved redhead.

There's joy in these walls. Sure, the paintwork was new, as was the roof and the carpet underfoot. But looking out it was the relaxed and happy faces of his pack members that stood out the most. Everyone was clean, relaxed and happy, and it was as though every smile reinforced how positive pack life could be.

"Alpha," Molly came over, her ever present son on her hip. "Robby's done with the roof now, you must come over and see some time. While he was up there, I managed to convince him to paint the gables, and we even have a new front door. The house looks lovely again and I can't wait for you and the alpha mate to see it. Oh, and the mayor called and said he'd be happy to attend the opening of the new homeless resource center next week."

Shadow grinned. Of course, Molly was more interested in sharing news about her new roof than the fact the mayor called. But she'd proven to be a valuable PA since Shadow learned that she didn't like working if it meant leaving her youngest at home. Now she ran Shadow's projects as efficiently as she ran her house and mate. "Rowan and I will make a point of coming over on Monday to see the roof and thank you for the message from the mayor. Are the contractors all finished?"

"Rowan's gran was over there this morning complaining about the mess they'd left behind. Her and her friends were armed with brooms," Molly said happily. "The keys to the building are on your desk along with the compliance certificates." She juggled the youngster on her hip who was staring at Shadow with wide eyes. "I'd better get this one back to his dad. See you Monday morning."

"That woman is the model of efficiency," Marco said as he watched Molly juggle her child as she walked away. "But I don't envy her mate at all. She rules that household absolutely."

"Which is why she's the perfect PA for us." Shadow looked around the hall again. "Where's Rowan? I thought he'd be here by now."

"He said he had to go down to the local council offices," Dominic said, leaning over and grabbing a large heap of meat from the platters that ran down the middle of the table. "Our shifter council got in touch this morning and said there was a wolf related incident in town, and Rowan said he'd take care of it. He had a meeting in town with that software company lawyer too, to finalize his last payment, so it made sense for him to do both things in the same trip. Talon's with him, so he won't get into trouble."

"Ooh, he's getting the final payment," Rutig waved his glass in Shadow's direction. "What are you going to do now your sweet mate is richer than you are?"

Shadow chuckled. Yes, he'd been shocked by just how much money could be made from selling a computer game, but he knew for a fact an increased bank balance wasn't going to change his mate's loving nature. "I think he plans on revamping more rooms at the pack house," he said. "Apart from that, I can't see anything else changing at all."

He looked up at the ceiling as something in the back of his brain hummed. "He's coming. I can feel him." Shadow and Rowan still hadn't got a full mind link yet, although now Shadow carried his mate's bite, their connection was a lot closer. As Shadow relaxed more and more into their relationship, he knew it was only a matter of time before he let Rowan take that final step so they could have a full mind link.

Looking over to the doors, he saw Rowan coming in, a nervous look on his face, with Talon behind him. Shadow frowned as he noticed Talon was carrying Rowan's satchel and Rowan had two baby shaped bundles in his arms. He got out of his chair, weaving through the tables effortlessly, keen to find out what was going on. Rowan's smile was just as open as it always was, but Shadow could see the worry in his eyes.

/~/~/~/~/

"Hi, hon," Rowan smiled up at his mate, his heart warmed as always just from seeing him.

"I'm glad to see you too," Shadow dropped a kiss on his head, but of course, he wasn't going to ignore the babies Rowan was holding. "What do we have here? Something to do with the council issue, I take it?"

Rowan nibbled his bottom lip, and then looked around at all the people who were watching them. "Can we duck out for a minute. I'd like to talk to you."

"You're not taking those youngsters out in the cold again," Talon said grumpily. "They need feeding, we've still got to find cots for them, and my hands are still sore from working out how to install blooming car seats. It's simple." To Rowan's shock, Talon plucked Cynthia out of his arms, and put her in Shadow's, who clutched and supported her instinctively.

"Congratulations Alpha. Thanks to your mate's quick advocacy skills, you're a daddy. Now, I hope someone saved me a damn plate, because the alpha mate does not understand that someone with my awesome nature needs feeding regularly."

Rowan hung onto Cian, rocking him gently as he studied Shadow's face.

"We're parents?" Shadow touched Cynthia's blanket gently with one finger, pushing back the cover so he could see her sleeping face. "I thought you were just going to pick up the last of your money."

Rowan shuffled between his good leg and his bad leg, trying to ease the ache. "Well, yes, I was, but then our council called, and told me to get down to the local council offices. There'd been this car accident just outside of town." Rowan felt his tears well up as he thought about what he'd been told. "The parents are dead, and they were lone wolves, coming here because they'd heard how well this pack was doing, and the local council wanted to put them in a

303

home, but our council couldn't allow that because..."

"Because they're shifters. I understand," Shadow said gently, rocking Cynthia who'd started to stir. He had no idea how natural he was with children and Rowan felt a stir of hope.

"I had to sign for custody of them," he said anxiously. "Our council representative was there trying to make things easier, but the local council said if no parents could be found, then they'd have to go into state care until someone could take them. And I just knew that would take too long. I mean, look at them."

"We have custody of them, permanently?" Rowan's heart leaped at Shadow's use of the word 'we'.

"We're on trial for now, for a month, because the local council wasn't happy that you and I weren't married, and with us both being men and everything, but then the mayor came through, and he knew how much you're trying to do with the homeless, so he put his two cents in.

The pack house will have to be remodeled, and I was hoping Gran would..."

"We'll handle it. All of it." Shadow nudged Cynthia around so she rested on his broad forearm and dropped the other arm around Rowan's shoulder. "Do they have names?"

"Er, yes." Rowan nestled under Shadow's arm. "You have Cynthia and I have Cian. They're both four months old. According to our council, their parents were an alpha and omega pairing, and true mates."

"Cynthia and Cian." Shadow smiled and it was a loving smile that took in Rowan as well. "I guess we'd better introduce them to our curious pack members."

"You don't mind? About being an instant dad, I mean." Rowan couldn't believe how accepting Shadow was of instant parenthood. He'd been fretting about it the whole drive home.

"Your heart is always in the right place," Shadow said softly, for his ears alone. "You saw a need and you jumped in to fill it. I don't know the story about these little ones' parents, but we will, and we will make sure these little ones grow up knowing just how much they are loved. You and I, we have so much love to share, and just look at the table of over eager uncles over there."

Rowan looked over to the head table, and sure enough, Dominic, Bernie, Rutig, Craven and Marco were all straining their necks trying to see what was going on.

"And then there's your grandmother, along with her sister elders." Shadow nudged his chin over to the side of the hall, where Rowan's grandmother was chatting with her friends. "We won't be doing this alone. There's a whole pack willing to help us with these children."

"That's only because you were willing to help them first," Rowan reminded them. "We are all so much the better for you coming home."

"Just don't forget, I came home for you," Shadow whispered against

Rowan's ear. "You will always be my first love."

Rowan felt as though his knees would give way. But as he stood proudly beside his mate, while Shadow made the announcement that the alpha pair, were now an alpha family, he cast his mind back to the dark days before Shadow's arrival. *It was all worth it,* he thought. He'd gone from being the hunted one by Percy and so many others, to being one of the heroes in the story, and just as with any fairy tale that came true, he got his happily ever after.

The End.

You know what I'm going to say, don't you, lol. This was MEANT to be a cute little standalone story where Shadow gets his boot out of his ass and Rowan gets his HEA. But then I kept writing, and all these wonderfully unique characters kept flowing out of my fingers... I have a sneaking suspicion this is meant to be book one of a new series.

But it's not definite. I mean, you guys might not have even liked this story. Or maybe, you did think it was cute but didn't want to know about Shadow's friends, or if the grumpy Talon will ever find his mate. I mean, the bad guys are all in jail or dead, and the twins will keep Rowan and Shadow busy for a while. But as with all my stories, there is always something else going on around the corner.

If you get the chance, please let me know. A review is an amazing way to do it (and they seriously help me keep my pups in puppy food), but if you're not comfortable with your thoughts being public for all to see, then you know how to get in touch with me. I would love to hear from you. I had real fun with this story, and it would be nice to visit them again.

It's not easy for any of us to stay positive with all the stuff going on in the world right now. I hope, in some tiny way I've made you smile and if I did, please share that smile with others.

Hug the ones you love, my friends, and stay safe wherever you are.

Lisa xx

About the Author

Lisa Oliver had been writing non-fiction books for years when visions of half dressed, buff men started invading her dreams. Unable to resist the lure of her stories, Lisa decided to switch to fiction books, and now stories about her men clamor to get out from under her fingertips. With over fifty MM true mate titles to her credit so far, Lisa shows no sign of slowing down.

When Lisa is not writing, she is usually reading with a cup of tea always at hand. Her grown children and grandchildren sometimes try and pry her away from the computer and have found that the best way to do it is to promise her chocolate. Lisa will do anything for chocolate.

Lisa loves to hear from her readers and other writers (I really do, lol). You can catch up with her on any of the social media links below.

Facebook –
http://www.facebook.com/lisaoliverauthor

Official Author page –
https://www.facebook.com/LisaOliverManloveAuthor/

My new private teaser group - https://www.facebook.com/groups/540361549650663/

And I am now on MeWe – you can find my group at http://mewe.com/join/lisa_olivers_paranormal_pack

My blog - (http://www.supernaturalsmut.com)

Twitter – http://www.twitter.com/wisecrone333

Email me directly at yoursintuitively@gmail.com.

Other Books By Lisa/Lee Oliver

Please note, I have now marked the books that contain mpreg and MMM for those of you who don't like to read those type of stories. Hope that helps ☺

Cloverleah Pack

Book 1 – The Reluctant Wolf – Kane and Shawn

Book 2 – The Runaway Cat – Griff and Diablo

Book 3 – When No Doesn't Cut It – Damien and Scott

Book 3.5 – Never Go Back – Scott and Damien's Trip and a free story about Malacai and Elijah

Book 4 – Calming the Enforcer – Troy and Anton

Book 5 – Getting Close to the Omega – Dean and Matthew

Book 6 – Fae for All – Jax, Aelfric and Fafnir (M/M/M)

Book 7 – Watching Out for Fangs – Josh and Vadim

Book 8 – Tangling with Bears – Tobias, Luke and Kurt (M/M/M)

Book 9 – Angel in Black Leather – Adair and Vassago

Book 9.5 – Scenes from Cloverleah – four short stories featuring the men we've come to love

Book 10 – On the Brink – Teilo, Raff and Nereus (M/M/M)

Book 11 – Don't Tempt Fate – Marius and Cathair

Book 12 – My Treasure to Keep – Thomas and Ivan

Book 13 – is on the list to be written – it will be about Wesley and yes, he will find his mate too, but that's all I can say about this one for now ☺ (Coming soon)

The Gods Made Me Do It (Cloverleah spin off series)

Book One - Get Over It – Madison and Sebastian's story

Book Two - You've Got to be Kidding – Poseidon and Claude (mpreg)

Book Three – Don't Fight It – Lasse and Jason

Book Four – Riding the Storm – Thor and Orin (mpreg elements [Jason from previous book gives birth in this one])

Book Five – I Can See You – Artemas and Silvanus (mpreg elements – Thor gives birth in this one)

Book Six – Someone to Hold Me – Hades and Ali (mpreg elements but no birth)

The Necromancer's Smile (This is a trilogy series under the name The Necromancer's Smile where the main couple, Dakar and Sy are the focus of all three books – these cannot be read as standalone).

Book One – Dakar and Sy – The Meeting

Book Two – Dakar and Sy – Family affairs

Book Three – Dakar and Sy – Taking Care of Business

Bound and Bonded Series

Book One – Don't Touch – Levi and Steel

Book Two – Topping the Dom – Pearson and Dante

Book Three – Total Submission – Kyle and Teric

Book Four – Fighting Fangs – Ace and Devin

Book Five – No Mate of Mine – Roger and Cam

Book Six – Undesirable Mate – Phillip and Kellen

Stockton Wolves Series

Book One – Get off My Case – Shane and Dimitri

Book Two – Copping a Lot of Sin – Ben, Sin and Gabriel (M/M/M)

Book Three – Mace's Awakening – Mace and Roan

Book Four – Don't Bite – Trent and Alexi

Book Five – Tell Me the Truth – Captain Reynolds and Nico (mpreg)

Alpha and Omega Series

Book One – The Biker's Omega – Marly and Trent

Book Two – Dance Around the Cop – Zander and Terry

Book Three – Change of Plans - Q and Sully

Book Four – The Artist and His Alpha – Caden and Sean

Book Five – Harder in Heels – Ronan and Asaph

Book Six – A Touch of Spring – Bronson and Harley

Book Seven – If You Can't Stand the Heat – Wyatt and Stone (Previously published in an anthology)

Book Eight – Fagin's Folly – Fagin and Cooper

Book Nine – The Cub and His Alphas – Daniel, Zeke and Ty (MMM)

Book Ten – The One Thing Money Can't Buy – Cari and Quaid

Book Eleven – Precious Perfection – Devyn and Rex

Spin off from The Biker's Omega – BBQ, Bikes, and Bears – Clive and Roy

There will be more A&O books – This is my go-to series when I want to have fun.

Balance – Angels and Demons

The Viper's Heart – Raziel and Botis

Passion Punched King – Anael and Zagan

(Uriel and Haures's story will be coming soon)

Arrowtown

A Tiger's Tale – Ra and Seth (mpreg)

Snake Snack – Simon and Darwin (mpreg)

Liam's Lament – Liam Beau and Trent (MMM) (Mpreg)

Doc's Deputy – Deputy Joe and Doc (Mpreg)

NEW Series – City Dragons

Dragon's Heat – Dirk and Jon

Dragon's Fire – Samuel and Raoul

Dragon's Tears – (coming soon)

Standalone:

Rowan and the Wolf – Rowan and Shadow (series to be determined by reader vote)

Bound by Blood – Max and Lyle – (a spin off from Cloverleah Pack #7)

The Power of the Bite – Dax and Zane

One Wrong Step – Robert and Syron

Uncaged – Carlin and Lucas (Shifter's Uprising in conjunction with Thomas Oliver)

Also under the penname Lee Oliver

Northern States Pack Series

Book One – Ranger's End Game – Ranger and Aiden

Book Two – Cam's Promise – Cam and Levi

Book Three – Under Sean's Protection
– Sean and Kyle – (Coming soon)